AMATEUR

PEOPLE

Andrée Connors

FICTION COLLECTIVE   NEW YORK

First Edition

Copyright © 1977 by Andrée Connors
All rights reserved

Library of Congress Catalog No: 76-47836

ISBN: 0-914590-30-8 hardcover
ISBN: 0-914590-31-6 paperback

Published by FICTION COLLECTIVE

Distributed by George Braziller, Inc.
One Park Avenue
New York, N.Y. 10016

This publication is in part made possible with support from the New York State Council on the Arts, Brooklyn College, and Teachers and Writers Collaborative.

AMATEUR PEOPLE

For Don and Piper

part one/ **Lame Excuses From The Innocent**

If life's a billiard ball, why not put a little english on it? That's what she said, can you bear it? So I pointed out a why not or two: You might end up in a wrong pocket, I said. You might miss the ball entirely. Why, you might even rip your felt. Rip your felt . . ."

The old man in the tophat nodded as he spoke into the falling snow, talking to himself in the night. Perched on a pile of boulders, he might've been some mass-produced god in a neglected shrine, or a falcon in formal tatters, waiting.

11

He absentmindedly rubbed his finger on the frayed edge of his lapel.

"Yessir. A lot of 'em end up in wrong pockets and wonder how the hell they got there . . . huddled in some dusty deadend hole. Hear that, all you flakes? Better watch out, drifting around the way you do . . . you might end up in some miserable crevice, stuck . . . aim for the top, my lads, seen too many crevice-dwellers as it is. Had it. Come on now, see how many of you have the skill and nerve to land right here beside me . . ."

He snorted in disgust.

"Mindless little beasts, look at you. Landing every which way. You'd make lousy pool players, I'll tell you that, my crystalline lazies, lousy. Not a shrewd one among you. No hustler potential. Look at you. Can't even get a rise out of you. Just swallowing my insults like mother's milk. Milquetoasts and rogues . . . what a sad affair this world is . . . sad. Where're the mead halls and gallant men now, I ask you? Where's straightforward rational thought these days, eh? Where's Logos? I'll tell you where! *Eaten.* They're all in the stomachs of wallydrags and mollycoddles. That's where. Ignominiously digesting and becoming great moronic turds. That's what. Is there a man among you—snowflakes! damn you, listen to me!—is there a man in your midst who's an exception to this pathetic rule? Eh? Logos-eaters! Courage-crunchers!"

He paused.

"Is there a King Arthur up there, hidden among you serfs? A free spirit among you Babbitts? A Lone Ranger in the common mob? A Thumper in your vapid cabbage patch? Eh? Look at you all, it's enough to . . . skydiving, cavorting through my night, trespassing . . . well, time to organize. Celestial spring-cleaning you might say . . . you're all spreading yourselves too thin. Gotta lump together—mass yourselves, boys—one big fluffy white snowthing, that'd be the idea, one big snowball, one thud down, no mess, no dispersion, no lack of focus. This dandruffy dropping about won't do. If you all lack individuality, if you can't find a hero in your midst, at least band together."

Having by now worn all the threads off one-frayed lapel, he started on the other.
"No indeed. Doesn't seem all that complicated. Isn't. It's all the same thing . . . just alot of, uh, analogies on the loose . . . this is an example of that, and that's an example of this. A beer spilling off a table's just the Grand Canyon and—so on. Well. So you guys are dandruff. Flour sifting into a cookie. Get it? Not such hot stuff after all, eh? Cut you down to size, I will. Uppity. Stuck-up flakes. When you figure out how simple it is, you'll melt of shame. You guys . . . there's something to be done and there's a doer, so what do you do? You do it. Simple. A dart and a target—splat. That's all. A custom cue and an eightball—zip. Whack. In the pocket. Socko. And if your basic straight line from point *a* to point *b* is—uh, obstructed, well then you use your I.Q. and go around it. Don't whimper and give up! Circumvent failure! Avert disaster! Discover ingenuity! Stand on a friend's shoulders to throw your dart—hell, stand on his face if you have to. But hurl that dart! Crouch in a poolpocket, embezzle chalk if needs be, but place that stiped ball! If you can't do it straight on, do it at angles! Don't be dummies! After all, if life's a billiard ball, why not put a little english on it? Eh? Eh?"

•   •

A half-mile away, a young woman, Varia, frowned and tossed in her sleep . . . she was resisting a dream about neuro-surgery and christmas cards. She would've preferred the recurrent dream about her Iroquois ancestress: she'd grown fond of the dream image—an ancient woman wearing a wig made from a giant hammered nickel, with a dry wit and bagelcrumbs caught in the corners of her mouth. That dream always left her feeling alert in the morning. This dream was disturbing her, exhausting her. But some surface level of her mind reminded her that she was, after all, asleep in a giant cradle, so she slept on, rocking slowly in her boat.

●

Two miles away, two figures plowed their silent way through the falling and fallen snow, towards a landmark: the pile of boulders where the old man, Mouldie, sat.

●

"This is a morning. Capital M, you understand."
He whispered this to the captive snowflake in the palm of his hand. The flake didn't respond. The old man sighed as he used his free hand, which was gloved, to remove his monocle and rub off the condensation; the morning was so cold that his body heat fogged up the monocle repeatedly, and repeatedly he removed it and cleaned it off. It was beginning to annoy him, trying to keep his monocle clear and his snowflake from blowing away or getting bored.

"This is not just any morning. This is an absolutely CELLOPHANE morning imbedded in a, uh, velvet winter. Are you listening? Now look—inside this dawn are some footprints: see? White on white. Now if you'll notice, the prints are grouped like this: two small, two smaller."

He tipped his right hand up about thirty degrees, so the snowflake could see over the ball of his hand, and with his left hand (pinkie flexed) pointed to the path of footprints in front of him.

"They weave across each other at points, but in between these points, they're parallel in a rather companionable track. So. Do we agree that these are the tracks of naked human feet? And do we agree that it was not *our* feet which made these footholes? Are we in perfect accord about where these tracks seemed to originate? Given the limitations of a restricted field of vision, obviously. I'm not forgetting that we're dealing with a horizon, with all it's accompanying frustrations.

Well then. Would you say that we concur that these holes— side by side, small by smaller, cross by straight, began at the edge of the east horizon, crunched through The Great Plain . . . ah, softly, softly, in the owly night, my little sedentary friend, softly, then rustled through the minor forest directly behind us—here, right over there—"

(He turned so the forest was in the flake's field of vision)

"—small by smaller, as you can see, stepping round the griffin thickets, yes, then they pocked their way through the crusty meadow *here—*"

(A quick jerk to the right)

"—moonshadows in the snowholes! Deer sleep! And ended . . ."

(Another quick jerk to the right, which brought him back to his original position)

"*—at this bay's nipply edge?!* Ah."

He paused briefly, composing himself. He cleared his throat to bring his voice down.

"Can we surmise, then, that the last four holes at the water's edge are part and parcel of the entire string of indentations we have been discussing? And that it is most unlikely that they are one of Nature's freak coincidences? That it is not by chance that they match exactly all the thousands of other holes we have examined and remarked upon? Hmmn?"

(Here he looked patronizing yet slyly conspiratorial)

"Now, resting in the security of our logic, shall we tackle the next facet of our early morning intellectual puzzle? Hah? Very well. Observe if you will that there are two—yes, exactly

two—individuals standing upright, approximately three feet apart, at precisely the water's edge. Now . . ."
(A thought flashed: He was Albert Einstein, being Just-Us-Guys with a slow learner)
"—each of these persons is directly involved with two footholes, is he not? In fact, each person is actually *standing* in two of the final four footholes. So. Now. An easily overlooked but crucial point: we must ascertain whether the small individual on the left is standing in both small footholes, and the smaller individual on the right is standing in both smaller footholes, or is the small individual, in actual fact, standing in one small foothole and one smaller one, leaving the *smaller* individual also standing in one small and one smaller one?"

Without moving his head, or changing his expression, he darted a fast look at the snowflake. No reaction. He couldn't believe it, but decided to humor it since it had been his experience that snowflakes were often inscrutable.
"We should thank the lord for our mutual and keen powers of discernment, my friend. How quickly we computed the visual information afforded us. Indeed the *small* one is in both small ones, and the *smaller* one is in *both*-BOTH-smaller ones! Ergo—we can be reasonably certain that these two individuals are in actual, EXPERIENTIALLY CERTIFIED *FACT!* to hell with hypothesis! the selfsame individuals who made every bleeding set of footholes in that long pocked path. And to add frosting to the cake, I'll even throw caution to the winds and wager that the small one consistently made a matched set of small prints, and the smaller one—"

The snowflake shifted its weight, or rode an inch on a miniature current of wind; at any rate, it moved. Mouldie, suspended in midsentence, had won. The flake had conceded, run out of obstinacy, cried uncle, deferred to his superior intellect—it was ready to learn, Mouldie knew.
He took a deep breath and straightened his back . . . he had

agitated himself into an arm-flinging hunch and now, now he could enjoy the fruits of his work. He sat, lotus-style, on the snowcovered ground, setting the snowflake on his right knee . . . He adjusted his tophat (which had slipped back on his head when he was spinning around, explaining the footprint path), rubbed his monocle once again, and smiling coyly, whispered:

"Well, little fella, little flaky friend, I just hope I didn't break your spirit. Don't want to browbeat you, you understand, just want to educate you to the wonders of the world . . . about time we acted like true gentlemen and introduced ourselves to one another, wouldn'tcha say? Heh. Well. My name's Mouldie. Mr. Mouldie some people prefer to call me, you know how some folks don't want to get too familiar, never can figure that out though . . . call me M if that makes you more comfortable, all my close friends do, just M . . . and what's your appelation my boy? Uh, that's name, whatcher name, kid?"

Mouldie waited politely til the silence got awkward, then looked resigned and said,
"Well, tell you what, since the cat's got your tongue at the moment, I'll try to guess your name, and if I'm wrong, off-base as it were, you let me know, straighten me out, heh . . . I can almost always figure out someone's name . . . ."

He developed a shrewd expression, remembering the look he'd seen on buyers of used cars. Then he smiled.
"So it's Big Ernie. Glad to meet you, proud to have you as a friend."
Then as suddenly as he had become chummy, Mouldie turned solemn. He let out his words in slow ponderous chunks . . .
"Well, my wee wonderflake, my—Big Ernie, where do I begin?
No, no, that was a rhetorical question, I don't expect an answer . . . well, first things first. It's a big tough world,

kiddo, a tough world, and the younger you learn that, the easier it'll be for you. You're gonna have to work for every damned insurance coupon you purchase, sweat for every pair of shiny shoes you look at longingly, your innocent little nose pushed up against the store window, yes, sweat. You're gonna sweat you're gonna cry you're gonna bleed for those tapshoes, Big Ernie, I'd be selling you Pie In The Sky if I told you different . . . ."

He considered the snowflake carefully, then continued: "Well, maybe not tapshoes, perchance that wasn't the best example of the things you're going to lust after in your time . . . however, you get my point, eh? Look at me—I mean *really* look at me—do you think I got to where I am today without breaking my ass as it were? Oho no, my newly friend, I've made my mistakes, I've burned my special fingers—more than once I might add.

I've taken my knocks as they came, I've fallen down, reared up, endured infamy and insult, walked proudly through third degree spiritual assaults without a whimper, not me boy I'm no canvass, never a whimper no matter *what* came flinging madly out of the cosmic fan, I've tasted defeat and demurely declined seconds, I've savored success and upon occasion, I'll admit I lost myself and shrieked for more, which never endears one to anybody—sour grapes are the biggest harvest the world has yet produced don'tcha know—I've learned through the miseries of trial and error to apply the principles of draw poker to every phase of existence, speaking of which my boy, let us amuse ourselves with a bit of the cards one of these days, I'll teach you myself of course, uh.

As I was saying, I've seen it all by now. I've had my heart broken by loved ones who ate too many vegetables, I've watched helplessly while Noble Cretans took to wearing flashy watches and sunglasses, I've learned to respect Tijuana Dog Races for secret reasons I can't share with you at the moment, I've puzzled at the apathy of your brother snow-flakes, but now I understand that too, I've plumbed the mysterioso depths of the American stock market and come up giddy with the knowledge of my own power, having tickled its delicate belly and caused it to convulse more than a couple of times while I was down there, that'll show those puny bastards who plot against me, won't it Big Ernie, I've uh, learned the hard way, baby, the hard way. And now, I've got the chance to guide you, gently counsel you, answer your naive but darling questions about life, capital L that was, be the stern but patient father you always wanted.

And you? Maybe you'll give me solace in my advanced years . . . I can feel them coming on, you know, I'm not one to hide from facts. When that day comes, may I sometimes cry on your strong young shoulder? May I bury my worn face in your bouncy young hair, or bum, if that's not too bold? May I rhythmically tap my aged fingers on your sturdy knee when fraught with cares and afeared of dyin'? Will you, if needs be, be Bedpan Monitor—but no, I shan't wallow in morbidity. There's so much to teach you. What do you know of decimal points? Eh? How about penny sales? Controlling thunder? How would you defend yourself if accused of ignominy? And besides, what if they say bad stuff about you? Could you handle rejection in your present state? Do you understand why drinking booze and ingesting barbituates simultaneously doesn't make it? Have you memorized your family tree? And what about acorns and oaks?
Aha. Gotcha. You see, sweetheart, you need me.
Big Ernie—Big Ernie, ask yourself what chance you have without me . . . what possible future but melting into a common puddle with all your countless bastard brothers? How would you save yourself from the Ultimate Spring Thaw? Have you dared to think ahead? I daresay not. If so, you would've been quaking in your boots when I found you, not basking somewhat stupidly in the early rays of this very dawn. If so, you would've hunched up to me of your own volition, not waited for me to discover you like some would-be starlet. If so, you would've been studying a book, perhaps

practicing typing, making yourself fit with exercise, I mean there were a hundred things you might've been doing had you had foresight. However.

Things are as they are, qu'est sera sera etcetera so I guess there's no point in berating you now. Spilled milk and all. And the important thing is, my itsy friend, that I have chosen you to be my child, my SON. You shall not only have the benefit of my interest and experience, you shall someday, be you patient, inherit my worldly goods as well . . . to wit— these kid gloves, well, they're very nearly kid, such high quality imitation that no one but me would be able to tell, my tophat which needs no explanation, my monocle—should you develop astigmatism you'll find it comes in rather handy, hmmm. Yes. And I'll bequeath to you my own family lineage: the most important of which are my daddy and mum . . . Father, I'm ashamed to say, spent years searching for an adequate scapegoat for his failures, til one happy day when he realized it was easier and certainly more fun to produce me, then to continue his futile quest around and about the common world.

And start me he did, with the help of that sainted but pathetic creature, my mother. Mother, you must understand, was one of those women who—with each aching, solitary year that engulfed her—looked more and more desperately into her closet each night, wishing for yet dreading the moment when she'd see some strange man's fully clothed legs stumped among her demure dumpy dresses hanging there.

And sure enough, the appointed moment arrived: one Friday night, there Daddy stood, thinking himself concealed cleverly among this unknown broad's clothes, sniffing at them like a bloodhound—to hear Mum tell it fondly, years later— rubbing a rayon housedress over his unzipped private parts. Don't look shocked, Big Ernie, I told you you've got a whale of alot to learn, and we may as well start at home, much as charity does . . .

Well, one thing led to another, kismet being what it is you

know, and never were a pair of unhappy humans better suited . . . fulfilled each other's finest dreams they did. In fact, they had such a grand time playing peekaboo and rubby in the closet that they didn't get around to my conception for a good month. And strange as it may seem to your frosty ears, not yet being versed in the ways of young lovers, they consummated their love, that is to say they executed their first Majestic Bang, right there in their now-communal closet, finding each other between Mum's pale blue laundry-day shirtwaist and her Sunday just-for-best greyflannel jumper."
Mouldie looked at the flake:
"Heh, you little devil, hanging on my every word, aren't you? Haven't moved a muscle . . . well, you're off to a good start, Ern. Good listeners are worth their weight in rayon housedresses. It's little guys like you make it all worthwhile."

• •

Mouldie paused then and looked around . . . nothing had changed, it didn't seem possible anything ever could change in the frozen eternal instant he was sitting in. If the sun was creeping up the sky, it was doing so in a shifty backdoor way—the cloudcover was so solid and even that the light quality was constant, and there were no shadows to swing out and around.
Registering this, he was suddenly unnerved:

"GOOD HEAVENS, someone forgot to wind Time! Look for yourself, the sky! Here I am babbling on and spilling all my family secrets to your innocent ears, and all the while, there seems to be no while at all! Time's gone! They forgot to—the fools! Now, there's no Tickety Tock, no noon! However, and consider this an aside, you'll note that even in

21

the midst of an urgent situation like the present one, a *crisis* even, I'm keeping the presence of mind to attend to your learning process, your mind-expansion . . . because there's a lesson in here for you—Never Delegate Authority Without Apprehension, possibly subtitled Domestic Help Isn't What It Used To Be Is It?—or maybe even Time Flies. Consider the ramifications of this invisible tragedy, Big Ernie . . . ."

Here Mouldie humped over and hissed in the general direction of the snowflake's presumed ear, enunciating each word carefully.

"Three-minute eggs will no longer be a sane thing to order. *I'll meet you at the Ritz at eight* will be a throwaway nonsense line. *I haven't got time for that* will no longer be a polite excuse but the boring utterance of the obvious. Litter bins will clog with useless plane, train, and bus schedules—do you see where it will all end? Vermin will breed in the refuse schedules like there's no tomorrow, forgive me, I hate puns too, streetsweepers will quit their jobs in disgust, and could you blame them? I'm aghast.
Just think . . . we're sitting here exchanging cozy intimate notes and—wouldn'tcha know?—catastrophe strikes! Bet you just had the same word-association thought I did, eh? San Francisco earthquake, am I right? *Eh?* Think of it, hundreds of people must've been just starting to take their morning elimination, and with the first grunt:
THE WORLD ALL FALLS DOWN.
Only goes to show that all those clearminded toddlers who panic at their first sight of a potty-seat have a damn good idea of the risk they're taking, eh? Hmmn? *They're* no dummies, *they* know you never know when Chicken Little will be vindicated . . . .
O God. Can I bear it? Poetic justice is just too exhausting. If it's not one calamity it's another . . . I could tell you stories—never mind, we've got enough on our mutual hands as it is, don't we?"

Mouldie peered closely at the snowflake.

"Not going to turn sullen on me now, are ya fella? Hm? Scared? Is that it?"

Mouldie sat up straight again, trying to look expansive— "Nothing to be afraid of as long as Old Mouldie's around, bouncing you on his knee . . . this Time Crisis, this Anti-Minute Epidemic as it were, is just another memo in my IN box, so to speak, just another bit of Business Trivia that I have to deal with—every day this kind of thing goes on, amazing as that may seem to you . . . so it's nothing to get excited about, I just have to slog through it now or later, so I may as well—WAIT. That's *it*. Now there *is* no later, so if we shelve it for now—like they say in advertising agencies when *they've* got a sticky problem—we'll never have to do anything about it! The perfect wrap-up! The Final Solution!

You see? *Nothing* is too big for he who thinks. A bit of reason, a dash of imagination, a moment to let it rise in very warm air, and there you are . . .! A conclusion. You'll get the hang of it in no time, my delicate dimply. Soon you'll be turning them out yourself—one after the conclusive other, tumbly tumbly, just like popovers. It might be well for you to remember the words my dear mother embroidered on the sampler that she gave to my father for christmas one long-ago year:

CONFUSIONS AN ILLUSION
THATS FULL OF CONTUSIONS
★ THUS ★
ITS A WISE MAN INDEED WHO
JUMPS TO CONCLUSIONS

Do you understand what I'm telling you, Ern? Are you beginning to see the graceful hopscotch logic to life? Do you see how time eventually made me shrewd? —so shrewd that I've finally outwitted Time, our late and sainted dimension, itself? —which is only a classic case of the student conquering the teacher, a case of genuine—if traditional—revolution! Look around you, boy: the world's full of crazy-eyed anarchists and prophets of doom or nirvana—depending on the particular brand of soap they're selling. Yes, wild-eyed crazies, and *they're* called revolutionaries! Well, they're not. No. Do you know who, besides me, the Real Guys are? I'll tell you. A true bloodthirsty revolutionary is a suburban shoe salesman who wins at Monopoly.

Yessir, this is the man who's after my heart. He comes home from a miserable day selling mediocre merchandise and plunges into vicious combat with his wife and family.

He doesn't waste himself on the world. His energy, his cunning, his incredibly intricate maneuvers are used to build an empire in his own living room—where it counts! Where reality lies! He's at the heart of the matter, don't you see? He can, in one evening, through cleverness and maybe just a little deceit, be J. Paul Getty! If EVERY MAN conquered his world in his living room—or den, or rumpus room, or whatever, every night, the world would be changed. As long as they kept playing Monopoly, kept winning, they'd all be winners, all be filled with the nectar of power!

Now, do you see the revolutionary aspects of this!? This small shoe salesman plots and plans—and accomplishes—the nightly overthrow of his unknown economic superiors! The fact that they're unaware of it only validates his triumph further! It takes one hell of a subtle revolution for the vanquished incumbents not to even notice. All depends on which side of the proverbial coin—or Monopoly board—you're on, eh?

If on the bottom, you've gotta watch like a badger for the opportunity to present itself, watch for the moment to subtly revolt . . . .

If on top, you gotta watch like an eagle, so that when a subtle

revolt starts, you can swoop down and make mincemeat of it. Either way, be you badger or eagle, or snowflake even, you must pay attention or you're a goner.
Goner.
Told you it's a tough world, kiddo. However, and I say this with such humility that to an untrained eye it might look like pride, if you but follow my advice and example, you will tread the path of righteousness and success with nary a stumble. For instance you will notice that I not only have told you to notice things, I myself follow my advice and notice stuff.

I've noticed that you're littler than me. I've noticed that Time has stopped. I've noticed that your basic personality type seems to be Introvert rather than Extrovert. I've noticed that the whole time we've been chatting and getting to know one another, two weirdos have been lurking about the beach listening. And you'll remember I noticed their track of footprints some time ago . . . you'll notice that not only have they listened to everything we've said up to now, they are, even at this very instant, straining to hear every word. In fact, it's an example of Life's Little Paradoxes that their noticing us is eavesdropping, and our noticing them is Paying Attention To Life."

•   •

Then putting the snowflake back into the hollow of his hand, Mouldie clapped his hand shut, and whispered into his closed fist:
"Sorry if I seem abrupt, my sensitive pet, but I must protect you—even over your possible objections—from the insatiable curiosity of the public riffraff. Which these two pitiable

creatures may or may not be. Riffraff. That is. But I always say, When In Doubt, Hide Your Snowflake."

Mouldie unfolded from his lotus position with some difficulty, being stiff with cold and age, and then stood up with one heaving lurch. Looking steadily at the two figures at the water's edge, a few yards away from him, or rather: staring suspiciously at their backs, he removed his tophat, placed the snowflake on the bald top of his head, replaced his hat, drew himself up to his full height, pointed an index finger at their turned backs, and announced:

"Putting one's ear to the wall and one's eye to the keyhole, as it were, will get you nowhere with me, my good folks. If I catch you listening in, which I obviously have done, caught you that is, you stand the risk of enduring my considerable wrath . . . which I would right now unleash on you were I not in a benevolent mood. Lucky you, my frightened and contrite people. Lucky. Funny thing is, had you sidled up to me with a bit of obsequious charm, I would've gladly brought you into the conversational circle . . . I would've gener—"

"Stuff it, you old bag of wind."
The old woman, the taller of the two figures, spit her words over her shoulder, then turned away again.
"Madam." Mouldie seemed offended but composed.
"Madam, there are just two things more disgusting than eavesdropping. The first is for the eavesdropper to tell the eavesdroppee to stuff it, and the second is for a woman of your advanced years to be seen in any state of undress. It's horrifying, Madam. And to witness you totally nude would be less distressing than to see you as you presently are. Really, my dear old shrivel, that bit of lace that dangles in front of your antique groin simply doesn't . . ."
He trailed off, not knowing why.

The old woman crouched down, apparently ignoring Mouldie again . . . her long bony fingers, covered with ivory and opal rings, flashed among the pebbles around her feet. Every few seconds, one hand would make a quick, impatient poke at her hair which was wisping around her withered face and shoulders, then would resume its search on the ground. Her companion, a child of about four, had crouched down with her, and was playing with the filigreed ice at the water's edge, seeming unconcerned with both the old woman and Mouldie, who was now peering at the child with interest bordering on fascination. Mouldie's eyes and thoughts travelled over the child, picking up speed as they went:

Good God, can my old remarkable eyes be deceiving me? Or could it be my birthday, has someone parcel-posted me a Goodie? Perhaps that rude shrunken thing is the Goodie's keeper. Well then, I'll purchase a new one for him, he deserves something better than that system of ruin he's with . . . good heavens, the little squeezie's skin is veritably translucent, a see-through meat-wrapper, that's just what: lunar-beam flesh! I simply can't stand it . . . a tasty toddler, tipping into puberty not a minute too soon as far as I'm concerned . . . o, ringlet tumbles, o delight, midnight hair, black and sudden! His wee eyes piercing through a glitter and a shine, peeking through his mane! A cupidic smile—love's weapon of sweet destruction! Dimpled elbows to torture my bittersweet fantasies. Tickle.
His breasts! More than budding, a full mouthful they'd be! O God they approach ample! Not possible but true. Belly, classically round, buttoned in the middle, a velvet cushion for my weary but appreciative head, a succulent bouncy place for my eager lips.
O smack.
O sweet Jesus, would you look—the babe is positively well hung, lookit that stickapoo. That child has a formidable rod! If it's gargantuan while off-duty can you just imagine—I could faint. Now how does his see-through type skin bear the weight of those glorious globes, those ballsies, dangling?? With care and attention they could eclipse his bummy

. . . shall I faint? No! But it can't be! O Mummy and Daddy would you peek at this amazement! I musn't shriek. No I won't. This angel is equipped with every deluxe option and I may die. It's more than—cunt, he has a cunt, it just winked at me when he bent over, it did, it does, he does, a cherried jubilee, o happy birthday to me—"

The woman found what she had been searching for—a smooth white stone. She stared at it fiercely and mumbled: "A loss is close at hand . . ."
In one twisting motion that was simultaneously standing and turning, she faced Mouldie. Her gaze—intense, obsessive—hooked into him like the talons of a bird.
"Old man, listen to this stone. Imitate it. Live like it, with it, because of it . . . just as if you could."
She stepped toward Mouldie and thrust the stone into his breast pocket.
"As if you dared.Hah."
"Madam, get this rock off me!"
He tried unsuccessfully to stare her down, to get his attention back to the child. He tossed the stone over his shoulder like salt.
She paused then, considering the shabby old man.
"I've seen the likes of you, old fool. Oh, I've seen. Clearer than I've seen the loss. Til now. Now I see the loss as well, too clearly, oh ho, too, and it breaks me, breaks the shell."

"Madam, you're jabbering. I didn't realize you were mentally infirm. Therefore I shall generously forgive your previous eavesdrop—"
"Infirm! My mind. Yes. O yes yes yes. My mind doesn't care *if* you forgive, *what* you forgive, no no, my mind is too busy for that, my mind flutters *flapping* into blacks and screeches—hear me, old fool?—and out again, out into airs of smiles and soft sighs, and then back it slaps into bogs and caves where the loss waits, breathing. Whispers follow me there, back and forth, they're busy too, you know, whispers

busy whispering: *we've broken you we've broken you . . ."*

The woman, who had stood so still at the bay's edge for so long, since just before dawn, was getting visibly more and more agitated. She began doing a series of gestures, repeated over and over again: she'd crouch down, tracing her fingers over the pebbles, stand abruptly, glance with concern at the child playing with the ice, pace back and forth quickly—five steps in each direction—like a wild animal newly caged, stand still and pat her breasts like a man absentmindedly checking his shirt pockets for a pack of cigarettes, and then begin all over again. Mouldie, shifting his weight from one foot to the other, stood watching her.

He cleared his throat.

"Please Madam, you're making me nervous. You *are*. I can't imagine what has upset you so, but you look ridiculous. Please stop at once."

She continued, mumbling bits of what she had just been saying, retrieving words like wind-scattered snapshots and glancing through them, shuffling them:

" . . . broken you . . . bogs and caves . . . too busy . . . screeches and bogs and smiles and . . . smiles . . . soft sighs . . . caves . . . busy whispers . . . flutter and old fool flapping . . . FLAP . . . breathing breathing . . . forgive . . . well yes well no . . . broken you bogs and caves whispers flapping—"

"Deranged. Ah well. There but for the gross—uh, grace—of God . . ."

She ignored him and continued her ritual. Mouldie chuckled quietly and turned his back to her. He raised his eyes and looked at the brim of his hat and stagewhispered:

"Big Ernie. Can you hear in there? If you can, you must listen to this poor woman. Forgive me for giggling, it's not funny, it's tragic, but she's putting on such a show . . . I want you to consider her carefully because it's a lesson for you—What Happens To People Who Listen To Mouldie When They're

Not Invited To Do So And Don't Listen When They Are.
Invited to, that is."

He turned back to the woman, who was just coming up from
a crouch and going into a pace.
"Madam." He watched her pace.
"Madam." She patted her breasts frantically.
"Madam, listen to me—" She started into another crouch.
Mouldie took a quick step forward and held her down as she
squatted, his hands firmly on her shoulders, his body
crouched in front of hers.

"My good woman, you must understand that this, this Saint
Vitus Dance of yours disturbs me greatly. C'est vrai!"

She stared at him with a blank expression, but didn't struggle
with his grip on her.
"You also must understand that I realize that this kind of
pathetic disturbance is a direct result of . . . loneliness
and . . . frustration. Yes, my Mum, whom you would've
loved, had a saying about it—as a matter of personal fact,
she, with arthritic, loving hands, fretworked a sampler for me
one christmas. What a dear. It said:

†

*A FRUSTRATED LONELY WILL END UP PRANCING
IN MUCH UNHOLY SAINT VITUS DANCING LA LA*

†

However, it's not hopeless, no indeed, your lucky number
must've come up today in that I'm here to help you . . . I
not only am able to diagnose the disease, I can deliver the
cure. Or the goods, as they say, heh heh."
She stared at him still, her expression unchanging.
"Well Madam, let me put it delicately . . . you touch mine,
I'll touch yours."

He took his right hand off her shoulder and held it in front of
her face, turning it so that she could see both its front and
back, like a magician assuring his audience that he has no

tricks up his sleeve. He wondered if she noticed the mended spot on his glove's middle finger . . . she stared at him, unblinking, unmoving. He lowered his hand very slowly, as though she were an animal he didn't want to startle or dehypnotize, while keeping his eyes pinned to hers in cobra-with-bird fashion. He spoke softly while inch by inching his hand down . . .

"I will perform a laying on of hands and thereby cure your unfortunate nervous disorder. I will with a touch recover for you your imagined losses. I will answer every question you are too shy to ask me. I will miraculously extract this moment from your miserable past and future. I will teach you a lesson you didn't know you didn't know. I will instruct you in the perverse possibilites of pseudokid gloves. I will examine your antique body without prejudice, and give you a free estimate of its real and present value. I will surrender to you my glove's virginity. I will watch for your inevitable fantasy and try to label it. I will tune you like the g-string on a fiddle. I will strum you unselfishly. I will tolerate the depths of your needs courageously. I will sacrifice my hand on the altar of your appetites. I will discuss magazines with you playfully—"
"—what?" But he would not be interrupted.
"I will explain to you the theory of anything you wish. I will exercise your unused muscles. I will give you the ultimate pleasure of pleasing me alot."
"—what?" But he was a verbal train going down now, unstoppable.
"I can make you feel like a woman, I can make you feel like a sponge, I can make you want to want me, I can deliver you to your youth like a telegram, I can deliver you to your death like a rose, I can raise you to life like a force-fed plant, I can raise your hopes out of the settled dust without leaving finger prints, I can recapture your old glories without knowing what they were. I don't want to know. I don't want your love, I want your gratitude. I don't need your consent, I need your hesitations. I don't need satisfaction, I need your

increased appetites. I don't need your concern, I need your attention. I must protect and serve you while I think of it. I must rule. I must eat lunch before one or I get a headache. I must render you placid or I haven't done it right. You must tell me what you like so I'll know next time. You must understand if I have to cancel the future. You must find a virgin spot on your body or mind for me to touch. You must unfold my secret childhood like an origami project. You must remember my words and forget the meaning soon. You must allow. You must not tell anyone or I'll deny this. You must not deny me or I'll tell everyone."

Mouldie's hand, having reached the low point of its travels while he was still warming up, had been held suspended in front of the old woman's lace g-string in an attitude that could only be called a limp beckon. Now it moved into position, a giant crane taking aim on a building to be demolished. Or as he saw it, his middle finger was a heat-sensitive missile, ready to zero in wherever the pulse was quickest, the flesh warmest. He muttered, barely audibly, "Pay attention, Ern. You are about to be taught a subtle but major lesson . . . one that will open more than a few doors in your meager lifetime, one that will smooth more than a couple of paths that your wee icy foot is bound to tread."

The old woman's eyes were still locked with Mouldie's. She wasn't aware of his mumble, but she was aware of the cobra-bird situation she was involved in . . . she wondered idly which of them was the cobra, which the bird, and if there was any difference at all between the two roles, and if it mattered if there was or wasn't a difference. And she wondered at the changelessness of this place. It was, impossibly, exactly as she had left it years ago. Or at least, it seemed to be the same. But that too was unprovable. And irrelevant. And even if she were totally lucid now, all the years of fogs and pains would distort any memory. She realized without the slightest trace of satisfaction or even real interest, that she probably *was*

lucid at the moment, since she was questioning it.
And she wondered at the child's patience. After walking all
night, and keeping the vigil with her at dawn—til the day
broke safely, an easy birth this time—standing so still . . .
and now absorbed in the ice and pebbles, apparently happy.
And yet, she was aware of Mouldie and herself. She could feel
it like sunlight on skin. She also wondered when her mind
would go back . . . not too soon, she hoped, it was so clear
out here. Anything, even this old fool, was endurable—for a
moment anyway—when she was free of the bogs and caves.

Look at him. (She saw herself thinking, crouching, waiting.
She dispassionately watched her thoughts go by, fluid and yet
erratic as river rapids.) He's wrapped up in this. He believes in
this, in it, the old fool really does. Just doesn't see the
loss . . . thinks I'm mad as a hoot, just because my body
makes movements he can't understand . . . probably thinks
people who speak Portugese are mad too. After all, they
make sounds, noises, he can't understand . . . I understand
him all right. I've seen the likes of him enough times, with his
mending and his smiling and his talk talk talk. Fill up the
holes with talk old man, you won't be the first one to try. Call
me crazy and obscene til the cows come home, but
remember—you're the one reaching for me, needing, eh?
While you can give me nothing but maybe a cough.
Going to cure my loneliness, are you? You *are* my loneliness.
You, in all your disguises, left room for the loss which left
room for today. And you would call me mad. Perhaps.
Perhaps. I wouldn't claim sanity anymore than I'd claim you.
So. Perhaps. Say what you, think what you, do what you
will . . . to me. If saving and ruining shadows is what you
want to do with your day . . . but bear in mind, if it amuses
you, that that child there, tracing ice and deciphering pebbles
so accurately—that child walks beside me, not you.
That child bestows its early breath on me, not you. I can
touch that child without leaving any mark but a smile. If you

33

could touch him, I shudder at the burn your touch would describe.

But of course you can't. You don't know what the mad woman knows which is that you can't. If you but tried, you'd go up in a vapor. This all matters so much, but not to me. Nor to that sweet child.

•

Mouldie's hand continued its slow arc down and forward, going under the bit of lace, landing where it was soft and dry. He congratulated himself on marksmanship briefly, then moved his finger half an inch to the right just to be sure. Feeling the bristly but sparse hair, he congratulated himself again, this time with more assurance. What aim, first try, haven't lost the touch, he thought.

Moving back, out of the hair and onto the soft flesh, he slowly made a counterclockwise oval—a professional scout to the core, noting landmarks as he edged along the timberline, watching for weather changes. Sometimes these late winter countries burst forth into a false spring, and he'd find it most amusing if this particular wilderness did just that. How fulfilling it was to witness new seasons. And how much more so, to cause them.

Now his finger drew a tight circle around the old woman's clitoris, and then lightly pressed it, like a button. No reaction in either the woman's face or genitals. He paused, considering, pressed it again quickly, then let his finger trail down the edge of one inner lip, and skip up the edge of the other, at which point, finding himself once again perched on her clitoris, he pressed it yet again, then bringing his thumb into play, he lightly tweaked it, the way he would've tweaked the cheek of a child.

In fact, the way he would've loved to tweak the cheek of that particular child playing nearby at the water's edge . . . he

glanced out of the corner of his eye at the child's rear end—
then decided he'd better attend to the matter at hand. He let
his finger wend its way down, traversing the smooth tiny
hillside—the image that occurred to him was that of an otter
slipping gaily down a snowy bank into a forest stream. Only,
and this struck him as very wry, this stream didn't seem to be
running. In fact, had the old woman not been in a crouch to
begin with, he was sure he would've gotten no farther than the
forest. But she was in a crouch, and her body was open to
him, and she wasn't resisting him at all, in fact, she was still
totally immobile, so his playful finger slid right into her
mossy hole. And immediately back out; he wanted to drive
her wild, which meant pacing himself shrewdly. To get down
to business too quickly would result only in her physical
release. The flourishes, the original tricks, the looming and
weaving of her excitement—that's where the art lay. When
she reached the point of total loss of perspective, then she
would be really his. And if she, as an old bird, took a bit more
work, that was alright—it kept him sharp. His self-assurance
now led him to see himself as the old champion ballroom
dancer, defending his crown, spotlighted and poised, doing
his perfect execution of the Digital Tango in front of the awe-
struck contenders. He hoped the child by the water and Big
Ernie were paying attention. He knew it was a rare
opportunity, seeing an old master at work.

He slid the tip of his finger back into her entrance and turned
slowly. A bit of moisture. He searched her face for some sign,
some remembered spark. He swiveled his fingertip steadily as
he said, "Why look so blasé, Madam, there is definite damp
proof of girlish excitement at hand. Let me lead you in our
little duet of physical intricacies and emotional explosions . . .
at least let me suggest that it soon become a duet, rather than
the solo pirouette I seem to be doing . . . for openers, I
suggest you let yourself show a trace of thrill, perhaps from
there you'll progress to my trouser buttons. My loins hunger
for your hand the way my hand hungered for your loins but a

moment ago."

He thought then of the pornographic comic book he had designed and made up for his mother, as a Mother's Day present, once . . . He strained to remember which part had held her interest the most. It was page 103, he was sure of it. So while keeping his fingertip inside, he let his other fingers skitter around the opening, letting his little finger wander towards her anus . . . he considered this maneuver his pièce de résistance, and he would've saved it for later but he was impatient as a child showing off, and he knew this would have to impress, or at least, affect her.

"Old man, my body has the habit of moisture, and I'm too old to bother about harmless habits. And I'm too old to bother about what you do to entertain yourself. Don't you know? You can neither harm me nor please me, and as for satisfying me—I told you, I tried to tell you, about the loss . . . that loss is so whole, so final, there's nothing you can take from me, nothing I can give to you even if I wanted to, nothing you can give to me even if you wanted to, there's nothing. Not now.
But I knew you once. I found you in some silvery bog, or maybe you found me in some midnight cave, I don't remember now . . . don't remember where. But you've forgotten me entirely. I didn't love you, I believed you. But maybe that's the same thing . . . what irony. I believed when I had so much to lose. You touched me then, too. Touched me and throbbed in me and welded to me like a comet—"
"MADAM I believe you're mistaken, we've never before m—"
"—*welded* I tell you, we became a burning planet, sizzling. I delivered over my truth, my enthusiasm, to you. Sizzling. Old man, you don't remember, but I convinced you of you. My surrender conquered your fear of impotence, and you rode me like a knight his charger—til the lungs of my belief

burst . . . and I collapsed, dead to you and dull."

The old woman was hissing this at him, rather than whispering or speaking. She was unaware that her fingers had begun scanning the pebbles beside her feet again . . . but she was aware that Mouldie's eyes had darkened as she hissed at him, and his polished smile now looked scuffed.

"What fear of impotence? Why you're senile on top of everything else, and lurid to boot. Just because I picked you up on a beach today . . . well, whoever it is you're confusing me with, God help him, but never once in my long and successful association with ladies have I EVER—audacious assumption. And stupid. And easily disprovable, your damned accusation, in spite of your viper's tongue. However, you might bear in mind that more than one good man has been seriously wilted by that kind of talk. Here, my lewd little asp, put your money where your mouth is, or uh, your mouth where your doubts are, and prove to yourself the condition of my Eight Inches Of Sheer Power."
He made an exaggerated fumble at his trouser buttons with his free hand.
"I know your condition." She thought he looked younger when angry. Probably it was the heightened color in his face. She moved her head from side to side, almost imperceptibly. A minimum but complete negation. Then she picked up one of the white pebbles by her feet, gently pushed the old man's hand away from her body, and dropped the pebble into his still upturned hand.

"Go away and listen to this stone. It sings of a law and a magic you don't know about. It knows that silvery bog . . . It might remind you of that time, even if you can't hear its stone-hum. Stone song. A Stonehenge reduction, that's what I'm giving you. Hah heh heh . . . ."

She ended with a cackle, and rocked back on her haunches. Her kneeknobs stretched her ricepaper skin to transparency

—twin ends of a wishbone eroding papyrus. Everything about her went from delicate to vaporous to improbable, and every movement of her body, every shift of weight, made the cycle begin again. She was a process of disintegration that kept happening. She cackled and rocked and watched Mouldie's face. Mouldie watched her watch his face, and rearranged his expression: angry frustration slid down into an imitation of affection and good humor. Then he cleared his throat and put the pebble in his coat's inner pocket. By now he had finally fumbled one pants' button open and was dramatically attacking the second.

The woman, although she still looked like she was cackling, made no sound. Mouldie thought: Purely visual sardonic spasms. Good grief.

Without moving his head or interrupting the action at his second buttonhole, he shot a glance to the extreme left—that child was still there at the water's edge, now bent over, scratching at the ice with a stone. The little darling's drawing. What an angel. What a bummy. So pink and bitable . . . then flicking his eyes to the far right, he made the second checkmark on his short mental list—first, child's busy, backturned, second, woods are deserted, all's well. Then rolling his eyes upward, skyward, he ascertained that indeed it was beginning to snow, gently but certainly snowing. He always checked any bits of movement in the air . . . at his age, he had decided recently, one must be on one's sensory toes constantly.

Then swinging his eyes down again, he looked at the old woman. Her eyes were focused on a spot of nothing about a foot in front of his chin; her eyes were glazed with boredom, hopelessness.

What's the point? Why didn't I poke him with a stick, why didn't I ignore him? Urgent things to do, utterly urgent. Clear obligations. Obvious last minute efforts to make. Why waste the precious—

(The third button had given way)

"And now, Madam!" He delivered forth, like a fragile fossil, like an antique manuscript that might fall to dust in the slightest breeze, his Eight Inches Of Sheer Power. He displayed it on his little finger, his cigar-wrapper pinkie ring glinting in the cold light.

The woman squinted against the snow, which was now falling steadily if softly, and stopped rocking on her haunches. "I even gave you a stone. Two stones, one thrown now, one pocketed. Just consider the loss. Yours too. Lord, yes. Go away, old man, you've returned to me a pain, a vacuum in a vacuum, a screech in a cry. And it snows besides."

"My dear decayed lovely, you gave me a paltry pebble. Now give me but a bit of head and we'll see some progress. Give you something to remember. Something to tell your bridge chummies about. I know you girls giggle about your conquests. Not much I don't know. I'll give you the ultimate pleasure—a mouthful of succulent Mr. Mouldie yummy. You might even judge it to be the only antidote to your feminine disgruntledness. You give me head and you'll find you've given yourself calm and tranquillity and a straight shot of protein. Fulfillment even. If you want a thrill, there's no time to kill. Do it to it."

The old woman looked at his cock. A fragile irony, she thought, even fails as a memento, it does. How could he have been my source of breath, my reason to breathe? This pathetic shadow just couldn't have stamped a midnight cave on my forehead. Fifty years. Sixty. She blinked slowly and said, "You see sheer pools of clear thinking, and choose to believe they're tear tools, wet weapons. You see snow and choose to believe it's aged eyesight. You've unlearned your life, even your infancy, if you had one. Of a sorts. You're now only a fool's seer, an idiot's ass, a fool's rear. That child's dimples make your mouth wet, I make you cruel.

You want me to make you a man, for all your hatred. Fear rules, indeed it does. I gave you a possible talisman, a salvation, and you called it a paltry pebble. I can give you what you want, my knowing mouth on your past-tense penis, and you'll call it inept. Only because of your own failure, and Time's. You fool, it's true, fear rules."

Mouldie looked at her blankly, politely. "If my manners were less well-bred, I'd refer to you as a hag. Being as they are, I'll call you Princess. Now, Princess," (his teeth were barely clenched) "that your hostile and bedlamish words are out of your mouth, perhaps you will put my Eight Inches Of Sheer Power *into* your mouth."

So saying, he shuffled up to a standing position and took a step forward into the V her crouched legs made. He creaked his pelvis toward her, and using the fingers of his gloved hand, opened her mouth by inserting his middle finger behind her wisdom teeth.
She looked up at him, pulled her pale lips back into a smile, or a grimace, cackled quietly, dropped her eyelids, and snaked her tongue out.
He entrusted to her tongue his pinkie's burden, and removed his finger from behind her molars. She sighed and drew his cock, in its entirety, into her mouth, and began to suck on it with obvious resignation and no enthusiasm . . . a ten-year-old sucking a throat lozenge while reading a schoolbook. Her hands were again coursing over the pebbles at her feet.
She sucked expertly. She smacked and tongue-tickled and pulled and blew and dampened and opened and closed like a sea anemone. She sighed through her nose. It was all so predictable, she thought. She opened her mouth wider and drew in his balls as well as his cock. Still, she thought, there's room for a marshmallow or two. Six slices of carrot. A pinecone on either side. Half a cup of whipped cream and strawberries. She dollied her eyes to the right as far as she could. Child's okay. How to explain this later. Another lesson

maybe: it's an ill wind . . . what's he drawing? . . . why'm I drawing on this—?

"Madam, you're inept. Surely you can do better. Why, my own hand could teach you things . . . why, my bedclothes, my own doctor-dentons, have proved more sensual in the thralls of a wetdream or two than you. Why aren't you doing right by me? You're guilty of the most profane sabotage. I ask you to go down and all that's going down properly is your stock. If I were a pimp, I definitely would throw you out of my stable of ladies of the night. Your stock plummets. Believe me, a life of vice would bring you only boredom and starvation. You have failed me, My E.I. of S.P. yawns. Ho hum."

At this, the old woman drew her head back, ran her tongue around her now-cracked lips, cleared her throat, scratched her left breast, and cackled. She blinked. She took a handful of pebbles in her left hand, and slowly and gently into his dark anus (which he often referred to as Loveybud), she pushed one.
Mouldie whooped and shuddered, and his dangling equipment jiggled with the spasm. The old woman blinked again. Another rock in the anus. Another whoop. Jiggle. The old woman bounced the remaining stones in her hand like dice, and blinked. Then another one up and in. *Whoop.* Jiggle. Cackle. Blink. Bounce. Up and in. *Whoop.* Jiggle. How's that. Blink. *Whoop.*

●   ●

She smoothed the child's wild hair and squinted at what he had written in the ice. He had embedded stones in the ice, making two neat lower-case letters and two periods . . . o.t. "o.t.?"
The child nodded.

41

"Occupational therapy?" Vehement headshake from the child.

"Outrageous tableaux?" Another headshake. "Hm. Outtakes?" The child nodded and pointed to the spot where the old woman and Mouldie had been. The woman pursed her lips, then smiled slowly. The child mimicked her. The smile evolved into a giggle for both of them. The giggle grew into hysterical laughter. The child pointed at the letters. A new typhoon. The old woman pointed a bony finger at the letters. They both collapsed on the ice-edge, immersed in hysteria. When the old woman finally pulled herself together, it looked like magnetic autumn leaves, white, heaping themselves into a pile. She settled and sighed.

"May the gods and muses deplore me if you aren't a Buddha," she said.

He smacked a kiss onto her knee.

"I've wasted so much of our time," she said. She stared over the water.

He quickly rearranged the *t* in the ice, and made a *k,* then tugged at her g-string. She looked down at him.

"Hm? o . . . k . . . okay, oh. A Buddha in the snow and light, ice and joy. Remorse melts beneath your smile. Lordy."

The old woman heard a murmuring, a pleading, strained and quiet. She turned around. Mouldie was again in a lotus position, buttoned up, propriety restored, forefinger outstretched à la Mickey Mouse, talking insistently, urgently, talking at his forefinger, at the snowflake that perched on his forefinger, at Big Ernie, who, it seemed to Mouldie, was being as taciturn as ever. Mouldie was explaining something, his attitude alternately depreciating, then earnest. Apologies and proof-clinchers. Press-agentry and autohype. Talk.

●　　　●

Turning, the old woman peered through the falling snow. She

scanned the beach-edge to her left and not finding what she was looking for, she tried the other direction. She knew it was there somewhere—it was pulled up on the beach, almost hidden by a heap of boulders. A rowboat. She was relieved, but not surprised. It was the final thing she needed from Life, and Life had usually played fair with her, on the survival-kit level. She realized that existence had a whimsical sort of justice, but justice nonetheless. Even when Life was coolly plotting the death of a day or a species, the Law prevailed. Granted, in all these years, she hadn't figured out all the rules, but then clocks and calendars had interrupted the lesson repeatedly—like petulant pets, or worse, predators in her life's forest. Distractions and disillusionments, snowballing deathward.

She glanced at the old man who was now apparently whispering a secret to the snowflake on his finger. He was making an obvious gesture with his free hand, and the woman looked away again.

"Of course . . . Stonehenge reductions fall beneath locker room lies. Breaks what used to be the heart. Glad it's near the end. The glitter of the loss . . . the gloss of the litter strewn through a life. The only sense that's stood the test of time seems to be nonsense."

She looked at the child, gently, like a blessing.

What a long way we've come. Through thickets and bristles and forever plains. Woods, too. He's patient. Not much longer or farther, and that's good. If I can just keep in mind the things I have to tell him. How I hate my old memory . . . sifts everything to powder and sometimes drifts of it blow away . . .

As soon as the woman had located the rowboat with her eyes, the child had started towards it. He was by now clambering over the side, into it. Once inside, he perched in the stern like a pudgy bird. The woman walked towards the boat, and with some effort, she pushed and slid it into the water, sprang over the side like a rusty but still taut coil, fixed the child with a stare heavy with significance, began to row, and said:

"Well, little one, a clock can taunt me just so long and no longer . . . I'm no fool, you know, I know it's following me now, sniffing at my tracks, defiling the snow with its lewd tock. I can feel it, my bones shrink at its hunger . . . hah. Let it snuff around empty footprints, let it rust in frustration at the water's edge, I'm safe for the moment, I've run for a lifetime for just this bit of business and no series of gears and seconds is going to rob me of it . . . How far can it be to the middle? Feels farther than it looked . . . damned old arms . . . if you were only bigger it'd be such a help. Well. You'll have your share of trouble and grief, time enough later. Just enjoy it while you can."

Then rowing in silence, she wondered: at what age will a clock begin tracking him? How exactly old must his eyes be to exude mindmusk? Is a hatching tock unwinding somewhere on his trail, following a toddle? And will his questionmarks feed it or hold it at bay?

I'm old and I've lost my answers . . . questions, questions, I have cancer of the questionmark, but what the devil is a questionmark but a bend and a poke, what the devil is anything but a bend and a poke, what the devil is that child sitting there but a friend and a hope for reprieve? But then again, what bending devil is that child, poking at my hope with his beginner's age and easy wisdom? What's a child anyway, but an amateur person?

I'm old and I've lost my answers . . .

"Are you warm enough, dear?" He shook his head but smiled.

She said, "Well, we're nearly there . . . ."

•   •

The rowboat sliced through the falling snow and the still

water. The only sounds were the creaking of the oarlocks and the sucking of the oarblades cutting the water. And the breathing.

The child trailed his fingers and wondered if they were going to ram the houseboat that he could just barely see through the snow. It seemed to be precisely in the center of the bay. Twenty feet away from the houseboat's bow, the old woman stopped rowing, dragged the oars, then pulled them in. Her arms were quivering from the row, but she'd done it, she'd gotten to the middle of the wintry bay. Like a successful pilgrim, she glimmered with pride at the child: "Now. Now, child, we're here." She paused to catch her breath. Glancing around, she absorbed the stillness, the silence. Just as she had known it would be, deserted and empty, waiting to be filled with the child's innate wisdom and her knowledge: the knowledge she would deliver over to him like a spiritual diplomatic pouch. It would've ruined her plans if anyone else were here and she looked around again, frowning and squinting.

Nothing. No-one.

The child searched the woman's face with his eyes, and suddenly understanding, smiled and winked slowly. He pulled his hand out of the water and leaned forward as far as he could, pressing his wet thumb against the old woman's forehead, between her eyebrows. The wet imprint froze immediately, becoming a white oval of flour, of moonsand.

The old woman ignored this, lost in her own mind. Mechanically, she straightened her g-string, pulled a wisp of hair out of her face, and aligned her rings, so that none were askew. She was catching scattered thoughts and tying them into mental bundles and stalling til she felt ready. Then a flash realization—she never would be ready, because she never would find a proper moment to describe failure; that moment didn't exist. She'd have to misuse a different sort of moment, borrow it, to fill with a failure-description. But how could she successfully present failure? A contradiction . . .

another muddle. It was River Styx. She steeled herself and waded in:

"Now. It's time for me to impress my past on your beautiful beginning, so you won't have to do it, too. Do you understand? It's been done, I did it, so you can go on to do something else. Anything else. Do you understand?"
The child nodded quickly. The woman eyescanned the bay . . .
"I lived here, right on this spot, once upon a time. In a houseboat. Listen carefully, dear, you'll want to be able to remember this later. Much later. Where was I . . . I lived here, on my boat, alone. Just for a small while. A short one. I learned some secrets while I was here. Most of them I didn't know I'd learned til I left. Then I knew. The wind and the feathers were the best part, you see—um, wait . . . well. I won't tell you about all the good times. You'll find your own good times, if they're to be found. You don't need lessons in smiling. But I'll tell you about the tears and broken things and clocks.
I'll tell you about the bald eye of the mirror.
I'll tell you about the choice of becoming a Person or a person, about the price you pay for not choosing bravely, in time. The price, of course, dear, is terror of your own name in an empty room.
I'll tell you about a pastel landscape of tin words and small fears that drag. I'll tell you about possible persons that melt together into a steaming quicksand porridge, and I'll describe dragonflies that get sucked down into it. I'll tell you how easy it is to lose the map of simple magic that you've got now, right now. I'll tell you about the hoax of the Final Solemn Answer—it has a thousand disguises and as many names, it's the watergod illusion of the thirsty, it will shimmer at you relentlessly. And the tarnished miniature dogmas that you'll stumble across here and there on the road, darling—don't bother even picking them up. They might or might not really harm you, but at least they'll weigh you down and tire you

out. Anyway, they'll rub a hole in your pocket if you walk far at all, and one by one they'll fall out. They fell out of my pocket, that's how I know, only they rubbed such a big hole in my pocket that eventually it was very little pocket and mostly hole, then no pocket and all hole, and now even the hole is gone. All I have left is a small scar in a pain, but darling, listen to my old whisper, because this is the secret: that I have raised this pain to pure art, to a torture of ecstasy, I've fed on it and given birth to new forms of it, in self-perpetuating rhythm. I am the Mother of pain, the Eater of pain, the Shitter of pain.

I am the orphanage door for homeless pains, I am the dark side of the moon, absorbing the whirling pains of all galaxies, I am the door-to-door salesman of the ultimate chimerical pain-brush. Do you see, darling, that each time I lost an answer through my tumbled gone years, I gained another facet of pain, I increased my capacity for pain, til now I am what I am. I had a brilliance, a genius, for pain, and I have fulfilled it beyond the possible. It has required a ruthless refusal of scar tissue, of sleep, of easy beliefs. It has made me a cyclops with a lidless eye, staring at the horrors beneath prayers and thanksgiving dinners.

But dear, with all this knowledge, this black truth, I haven't been able to tip myself into the light, I keep soaking up the cries of the terrible void out there, I am paralyzed with my terrible vision, although I know that I have seen more, breathed more, lived more, than those of common winking sight, still it's no comfort, because my vision extends far enough to see what truth is possible, what joy is possible, for those few with special sight . . . and you are one of those, of us, and you must go past me, past pain, past black, past past, you must soar into the third eye of joy.

Look at me! I am the consummate abstraction of pain, the art of pain, and only now do I understand the significance of it all—if pain doesn't metamorphose into joy, it just cancels itself out. Do you see? Do you see the joke in that? Do you see now that I am the joke? That I am the joke in grey shades of dying? And do you see that the point is somewhere in one of all the hidden prisms of before or after, and its laugh is lost among echoes of an epitaph we call Now? Do you see all that? Sshhh. Listen. Sshhh. *Echoes.* Echoes piled in a grave that I stump towards, gathering bits of the joke in my hand. Look at my hand: See? O god see me—I'm falling through my open fingers . . . I'm falling, deeper than pain—through shock and beyond—I'm disappearing in rattles—I am a rattle and—and—I echo in graves that you stump towards—I am a grave—o dear god I am—it's true—a rattle and a grave—I am the open hand I fall through—hearing my own echoes—I am a joke in grey shades of dying!"

•   •   •

He couldn't get her to move or respond at all. He touched her foot, her wrist, he stroked her hair the way she had stroked his, earlier. She just sat holding her hands in front of her face, peering out between the bony joints, her breathing muffled into her palms. Her hands were the only part of her that seemed solid; the rest of her still seemed vaporous, caught in a cycle of fog and rain and rivers. And now, as the child watched her, he read her position, her body language, as terror—but the next second, he saw it as shame, and then, emotionless acceptance of captivity in a finger-cage, then some state of consciousness that transcends labels, then bliss, then horror.
Her body was a kaleidoscope, her psyche, glass fragments that turned in chance patterns.
The child reached out again and touched the white ice oval between her eyebrows. He held his thumb there until the spot melted into a drop of water and rolled down one side of the woman's nose. He knew her spirit's pressure could only be expressed by tears shed from her third eye; and expressed only, not released, not cured. The old woman heard thoughts

somewhere in her mind. They were whispers in the next room, indistinct but urgent. The door opened slowly . . . My Undoing Was The Hearing Of My Own Words. Not the fact of them. Not the knowledge of them. Not the speaking of them. But the hearing. *I am a joke in grey shades of dying.*

The syllables had shattered her, shots into crystal.
The child had her knowledge now, all she could give him, so he no longer stood between her courage and the realization of her own destruction . . . the white heat of her awful vision had flooded in and melted her courage to nothingness, so there was nothing now to be dealt with or considered.
The door closed again. She was blank.

•   •

Looking past the old woman at the houseboat, the child tried to figure out if it was deserted or asleep . . . it was dark behind the lace-covered windows and the tin chimney was obviously cold: snow was building up on it. The boat—or rather, the shacklike cabin jammed inside an old steel hull— seemed neglected, but he decided there must be someone in it; it had a tension about it, the feeling of a pause between two activities, rather than the stasis of inactivity . . . the promise or threat of turbulence. Later. Soon.
He stood up, trying not to rock the skiff, and stepped in front of the old woman, turned his back to her knees, grasped the oars, and started rowing back to shore, standing.
Every few minutes, he'd turn around and brush the snow off her.

•   •

The skiff cracked through the thin ice at the water's edge and its bow crunched onto the shore. The child's eyes swept up and down the barren beach then stopped abruptly—there was a movement just beyond the group of boulders . . .

Mouldie was raising a wine glass in toast. He was sitting at a medieval banquet table: its carved pedestal legs were rooted in the snow, its top was becoming white and soft with settling snow, its elaborate setting (crystal, china, baroqued silver) perfect and empty . . . no food or wine, just snow, lining and rimming the various dishes. Set for two: Mouldie at one end, no-one at the other end.

Mouldie, every minute or two, would take off his tophat, remove his snowflake from the top of his head, say something to it—some observation he thought might interest it—then replace it and go on with his conversation with the no-one at the other end of the table.

The child got out of the skiff, and using leverage and determination, pried the old woman out of it, onto the beach. She stood in a half-crouch, her hands still over her face. He led her (he helped support her, she staggered and balked. She stumbled) away from Mouldie's direction, over the pebbled beach, through the snow, past a thicket of brush, to the beginning of the Great Plain. He led her to one spot, paused, no, then another, no again, then another; he found a place that felt right to him.

He eased her down and arranged her legs tailor-fashion, then running back and forth to the beach, collected pebbles (the whitest ones he could find) and dumped them in a pile next to her. After several trips, since he had nothing to carry them in but his hands, he began to make a circle around her, then a second one, then a third. Three concentric circles, the old woman in the center, motionless.

By the time he was done, the first circle was almost covered with fresh snow.

He wanted to brush the snow off her one last time but didn't want to cross over the circled stones. He hesitated, trying to think of some way . . . and not finding one, just smiled sadly at the vacant eyes, and noticed that the old woman's opal and ivory rings were now completely encrusted with snow.
Standing directly in front of her, the child made a sign: a Buddhist mudra, or pattern of the hands: 'the circle of the chain of causes', then turned and walked slowly back to the skiff.

And the old woman sat there, breathing into her hands and into her various deaths.

•   •   •

Mouldie, apparently still oblivious to the old woman and child, sat back in his chair. He unbuttoned the top of his pants, the bottom of his vest; spread his hands on his stomach, burped, and smacked his lips. The plates and glasses in front of him were by now full of snow. He thought, wonderful invention, brunch-by-the-sea. Nearly as droll a concept as heaven . . . not as dramatic as plague or as witty as vaudeville, but droll. Seagulls flapping. Air boiling with sunbits . . . veritably dripping yellow. Would that I had my hawaiian shirt with me. Leis and alohas . . .
(He sat back and patted his stomach)
Yas, makes a young man's fancy turn away from thoughts of plague, and towards fancy young po-po's prancing around in grass skirts and hawaiian shirts. And buses. Don't know why. Makes me think of buses. City ones. Must be the sound. A crashing surf and a bus pulling away from a stoplight. Same family tree, aurally speaking. Another wonderful invention, stoplights. Never get tired of pointing at them and making them change their colors. Little round rainbows. Blink. Blink. Blink.

Abruptly, he sat up straight in his chair, and spoke to the other end of the table.

"But enough slouching about for us, my friend! We mustn't drift off into idle contentment like so many cows . . . after all—life is not a cud to chew, it's a nut to crack. And crack it we will! Let's see. What'll it be today? Education, social work, philanthropy . . . done a bit of those already this a.m.— aprés morpheus, don'tcha know. Well. Responsibility's a heavy burden, it's all enough to bow my nimble back sometimes, but a job's a job.

And speaking of a.m., perhaps you'd say our After Meal Grace for us . . . you mustn't take for granted, you know . . . If you mind your spiritual manners, why, you'll have Pie In The Sky, delivered hot and steamy by a cosmic pizza man—but if you don't—"

(He paused and looked up at the sky)

"—then Chicken Little will indeed receive our apologies and assume her rightful place as a prophet. Posthumously, of course."

(Then lowering his voice and narrowing his eyes)

"So pray my friend, and make it meaningful but brief. I have sniffed at the perfumed air and sipped at the wine of available wisdom and I now see there is trouble afoot. Mischief abounds. It paddles, yes at this precise moment, it paddles and splashes into our immediate future. Out day is in jeopardy. Our marvels and awards are in danger of being tattered and trampled. How could we stand it? Trampled under the hooves of a wildfire . . . or uh, consumed by a wildfire. Come. We must dig a psychic trench."

●　　　●　　　●

The child tied the skiff to the houseboat.

part two/ **Problems of Small Gods**

Varia turned over under the quilt.

Behind a lace curtain, a child's face was peering in the window, steaming a small section of glass with every breath. She turned over again, her hair a huge tangle of darkness on the pillow, her sleeping expression changing from serene to ironic to irritated to pleased. She was dreaming, a final dream before awakening: like the last drink of the night swilled down at the door, as a bar closes:

A television interviewer was walking with her, trailing cables and cameramen, through a ruined castle. He was asking her solemnly, exactly how she felt about awakening every morning, and she pondered and thought and considered carefully, then answered him in a singsong voice, as though she had memorized the answer, having been asked so often. She saw no contradiction between the heavy pondering and the rote answer . . .

—Here is a morning. The sungod wakes me with a chill pantomime of his famous summer drumming, the first moment wraps me—ah gently tip toe nanny—in a robe of possibilities for the day, the dark nightworld of my unconscious, including cherubs and demons in equal measure— top billing being rotated fortnightly in accordance with the divine principle of justice—releases me, both spirit and physical baggage, to the barely-conscious state of private daybreak.

A bubble, I rise to the surface slowly, wending my way through liquid air warm and heavy with dreamlife, pausing as often as possible, stalling expertly, dragging my feet as it were, that is, as it would be if the concept of feet wasn't inconsistent with the bubble image that's central to this metaphor, the point is, hanging back is the procedure I'm talking about, hanging back to try to reopen negotiations with myself about the advisability of simply staying where I am, about two-thirds of the way up the liquid, or if possible, of going back down to where more of the action is.

Obviously, I'm a good if predictable loser in this daily battle, as is evidenced by my previous comment about the first moment wrapping me ah gently tip toe nanny and so on ad nauseum.

Then after flashing a practised smile at the interviewer, Varia awoke. She looked across hills of pillow and quilt.

"I hate the fucking morning."

"Aha. So. Finally back with the living, eh?" It was Mouldie, up from the chair he'd been sitting in, waiting, Mouldie,

hovering over the edge of the bed:
"See this stone? Looks ratty and sandy, eh? EH? ha. If you
ever achieve the internal rhythm this enfant trouvé has, you
won't need to ask me what's going on, which is what I know
you're about to ask, since I'm perceptive and you're *trés*
predictable, I mean, relative to my other friends who are,
every one of them, erratic and original if nothing else, which
is not meant as a how-you-say *dig* at you since if I weren't
rather fond of you—what the hell senorita I love you to
death—I wouldn't be spending most of my time with you, but
you sleepy little kruller, I'm *trying* to tell you something
about this stone, aren't I . . . I just found it. I was out at the
veritable CRACK of dawn while you were wandering around
inside your sleep somewhere, I was out on the snowing bleary
beach looking for Treasures, Surprises and Teaching Aids to
help you with, and this stone was just sitting there.
Now that's significant.
I mean things like that happen for a reason. A cosmic reason,
and this stone is here to teach you something about yourself,
with my help of course. So, as I was saying, if you ever
achieve the internal rhythm this stone has, ratty and sandy as
it may appear to you, you'll undulate in the cosmic flow,
you'll ululate, you'll hula—"
"Mouldie, get that stone off my pillow. Come on, please, it
smells like fishshit, I can't stand it. And why can't you ever
just say good morning. Not even say it, whisper it, really
softly, like this, *goodmorning* . . . "

Varia closed her eyes again. No. I'm not ready for this. Not
ready . . . my god it's so warm in here . . . I'm limp
. . . limp like yesterday's lettuce . . . bedded lettuce . . .
boat's all acreak, creak, creak, back and forth, constant
eternal creak, I exist in the great existential creak . . . water
thlurping . . . love the sound, thlurp, glup, miss lettuce your
creek's all aboating . . . your tin hull's arusting, arusting,
the seagulls are trusting, trusting and nesting on it, cold bay
surrounding it, rounding it, oyster guarding pearl, girl with

57

the solitary shackfloat, timberly rusty mudlark, madlark, madlark rolls, madlark knows the truth in flows and thumps and thlurps and in deaths that deliver newcries damp and new and churning, madlark knows the truth in sleep and giggles and leaps, in swoops that leave no room for moss clinging, no clinging but a clanging change, someday o let it be some soon day, a clanging change of madlarks whiting the sky puffing the air with thick creams of feathers, an only truth filling madlark with skies, an only sky filling madlark with truth, an only madlark filling skies with truth and feather and cry—

"*O no you don't,* I see you sneaking back to sleep, do you see this stone sleeping its life away? Is it flabby, pale, and lethargic, or is it tingling and alert in perfect stone poise, ready for anything? Varia? . . . *Varia.* VARIA! Answer me, is it flabby, pale—"

Varia sighed. "Alright Mouldie, alright. I'll get up." She didn't move. Look at him. A wreck of a vision . . . seedy, unkempt, unkempt hell, he's a ruin, fluctuating everchanging manifestations of—god knows what, creature of a thousand disguises, each one more ridiculous than the one before. Timeless freak. My friend. O stop: It's the damned Virgo in me . . . he's only trying to help . . . but *poised stone* . . . Is this any improvement on New York or L.A.? Why do I always—what's that old—jump from the frying pan into the fire . . . yes, but that horrid little astrologer in the Village . . . The Man With The Nasal Soul. Really the last straw.

He had spread her birthchart out on a formica table (it had stuck on a drop of jam, strawberry glue oozing through her twelfth house. He hadn't seemed to notice) so that they could both see it, and had moved closer to her, brushing her thigh with his.

'Well babe, let's see . . . Virgo rising, moon's in Gemini, sun's in Libra—that's an interesting combination in a woman . . . heh, why don't you hang around for awhile. We could go get something to eat later and, you know, we could get into your chart a little more thoroughly . . . no, really. Oh, for chrissake Varia—didn't you say your name's Varia? You have an interesting astrological make-up and far-out hair and I just want to get to know you, that's all . . . no need to get pissed off.'

'I'm not pissed off. I'm very bored.'

'No, you're defensive, babe, defensive. No need to get uptight.'

'Look, I'm paying you forty dollars to do my chart, Alex *said* you were very good, so why don't you just do the chart, I'm really, I'm just not, I mean, it's not just you, believe me, it's not just you, it's everything, this city's driving me nuts, the noise and people, I mean this psychotic cabbie was incredible last night you wouldn't believe it, a cabbie, and now you, I mean if *you,* you're really *into* astrology, and you aren't even aware of the feelings in the room, in a person, if you actually couldn't *tell* that I wasn't interested in getting into a thing with you, who can? Really, you've completely undermined my faith in you as a finely tuned sensitive communicant with the stars, o I don't know, all that shit, just forget the chart, fuck it, I'd just as soon spend the money on, on, I don't know, I've got to get away, everything seems like a cheap fraud to me, you and this bullshit apartment and the sidewalks, I just can't take the sidewalks seriously anymore, they're a cheap fraud too, I mean you see all those people, bankers and dental hygienists and well, everybody, walking along, taking the sidewalk seriously, they *believe* in the sidewalk, they *accept* going through revolving doors and back onto the sidewalk, and I guess I didn't expect you, *you,* to be like that, and you are, you really are, you do, you believe in sidewalks too, so just give me my fucking check back, and let's forget the whole thing.'

'Jesus Christ, you ask this chick what time it is, and she shows

59

you how to become a timebomb.'

•   •   •

Varia focused her eyes on Mouldie, who was still standing next to the bed, arms folded, sulking.

"Mouldie, what time is it, anyway?"

"It's precisely Now, my little chickadee." He'd been trying to learn sarcasm from Varia.

"You did W. C. Fields a week ago. I thought you never repeated yourself. Anyway, listen, I had this dream last night—"

Surprised that she had noticed his impersonation, he forgot to sulk:

"Subtle variations, my dear, always keep an eagle eye out for subtle variations . . . you'll notice my tophat is developing extreme patches and ragged edges right before your eyes, look closely and you'll notice that my cane is slowly getting gnarled and rough-hewn, that's rough-*hewn* my dear, my spiffy patent shoes have become veritable rags, flecks of foam and spittle are—"

"Beckett. You're doing a Beckett character. Listen Mouldie, that dream—"

"You're learning! The ignorant can learn! The blind can begin to see! The illiterate can develop erudition! The victim of massmedia can achieve humanness! My little guinea pig, I can see it's all possible—a world guided by nobility, finesse, and me—a world where laundromat kings in dented cadillacs evolve into shamans and seers, there is a pygmalion situation that's possible in its purity!

Billions of individual pygmalions, operating inside each t.v. fan, operating like spiritual plastic surgeons. The church, that old drag queen, will be exposed as a molester of children, the boyscouts can finally disband, Norman Vincent Peale will have to hock his pinkie rings, and I—I will jag around like a

60

proud psychic gardener, tweaking a cultural leaf here, dusting off a mystical tendency there, helping, yes, encouraging assuredly, but not doing the actual work! My clever little petunias will be doing their own growing, no more killer lichen, no more whimpering spanish moss sucking off oaks, we'll have no more of that! Just *fields of independent petunias and carrots!*"

"How nice."

Varia swung her feet down. "Christ it's cold in here . . . why don't you ever start the stove?"

"Because manual labor does not become me."

"Well, nor me, you pompous ass, but somebody has to put the coal in the stove and set a match to it. God. Now listen, do you want to hear about this dr—"

"It's *your* boat."

"As a matter of fact, that's true, it is, and if you're here that means you're what's called a guest, and if you have any manners whatsoever, you, as a guest, should help out a little. If you don't, then you're not a guest, you're a parasite. Killer lichen, whimpering spanish moss, mmm?"

"But what is this shrewing? This castrating? Grabbing at my ethereal balls with your coaldust hands? Is this why I knock myself *out* for you? Is this why I schlep around beaches at dawn to find teaching aids for you? So you can insult me? So you can crush my sensitive feelings with your common barbed tongue? Why am I here? Why? I hold in my sensitive, tapered, artistic hands, one of which has a double-jointed thumbknuckle in case you haven't noticed, *secrets of life.* SECRETS OF LIFE WOMAN, and I am TRYING to share them with you and you, like some common streeturchin, SHRILL at me about firing up a-a—stove!"

"Mouldie. I have been awake for four minutes. It will be half an hour, now, before I can drink one cup of hot coffee, since you didn't bother to put coal in the stove. I have not been able to find my hairbrush for *nine* days. Nine. I am getting tired of that quaint little coalburning organic stove, I'm getting tired of this picturesque houseboat, I'm getting tired of seeing you assume foaming-at-the-mouth Beckettesque characteristics, before I even light a cigarette yet, really it's repulsive, clever but repulsive, and I'm tired of your not listening to me, and tired of hearing myself sound so bitchy. Now besides all that, it bothers me that I don't really know what I'm going to do with today, anymore than I knew yesterday morning what I was going to do with yesterday, which means I will probably do with today ex*actly* what I did with yesterday, which was exactly nothing, if you'll recall.

Pouring my energy into a vacuum isn't my idea of a full life. I realize that I have no-one to blame but myself, but since I don't feel that I have much of a self left, lately anyway, that means I have no-one to blame but a sort of shadow. And any fool, not to mention psychiatrist, can tell you that to blame anything on a shadow is some sort of proof of madness. And you know as well as I do that I'm sane. Miserable but sane. The point is, when you harangue me and get me into . . . whatever it is you get me into—it just makes everything worse. I don't know. I feel like somebody who's colorblind struggling with a paint-by-numbers kit that has invisible numbers. I don't know what goes where."

"Well now, of course you don't you silly goose. What makes you think you CAN know what goes where? What makes you think any THIS should necessarily go any particular THERE? Maybe you're not colorblind at all. Maybe all the splats of paint are truly all the same color. Maybe the paintmaker did it to fool you. Anyway, who said you HAVE to put the paint on the canvas? At all? Why not paint yourself with it? Why not smear it all over yourself in swirls and patterns and have some real FUN with it? To hell with the canvas. Certainly to hell with the numbers. Where's your imagination? Eh? Where's your sense of humor? Where's your courage in the face of mass-produced paint-by-numbers kits? Where, now that I think of it, are YOU?"

Mouldie stabbed a finger at Varia. She pulled the quilt up around her, to protect against a possible second jab. "What do you mean, now that you think of it, where am I? That's *my* question, remember? You're the one who claimed —upon first meeting, as a matter of fact, to know the answer to that. That's why I invited you here in the first place, you promised to unravel the answer for me. Or, well, to help *me* unravel it, anyway."

Mouldie took his hat off and shook his head in discouragement.

"Mon dieu. Mon petite chou-chou. What circles you go in! Like a little bathtub duck that's wound too tight. I *am* here to help you, and I use everything at my disposal. To wit: the stone at dawn, our little Beckett guessing game, my general prodding of your confused mind, all the secrets I hold in my long tapered artistic hands—"

"I am not yet thirty, have known and loved some of the best men in New York, Los Angeles, and London, am a published poet and an adequate if unknown, well, not quite, but just about unknown, actress, and I'm sitting here in the middle of nowhere talking to an apparition. It gives one pause."

Mouldie slouched and tried to make his mouth droop.

"Varia, it saddens me so to hear you speak in that hardened and cynical way. My darling, you've become a corn on the toe of life."

"I beg your pardon."

"Callous. I mean a callous on the toe of life."

"Maybe I should go back to New York. I could learn to keep my mouth shut about the sidewalks. I could become a hairdresser. Maybe I could forget the important secrets that you have yet to tell me. Maybe I could forget that I ever wanted to know anything as—dumb—as important secrets. Maybe I could—"

"Enough! Close thy mouth like a pre-fab door sealing off uncertainties, lest they escape whining into the sunlit courtyard of Greater Truth. Open thy moist stainglass louvers, eyes don'tcha know I mean, and behold silently the scroll which I have prepared for you lo this very past night, a scroll with notes, comments, and wisdoms for your enlightenment, a scroll that emerged with me from the pulsating belly of a shrouded-moon night, a night heavy with omens and activities of the nether and near worlds, a night of uncertain parentage but definite destiny. Lookee here."

He drew from an inner pocket a rolled up piece of paper. He unrolled the first few inches and read:

"Notes Observations and Humble Wisdoms To Aid In Varia's Instruction Re Important Stuff—"

He snapped it shut.

"Ah, but wait! Before showing this to you, let me give you a word or two of background. These Notes, Observations, etcetera are the holy dregs, as it were, of my participation in the Intermediary Lunch we, uh, folk, held last night. A sort of board meeting you might say. In a different vein but in the same genre as the Elementary Breakfast and the rather more renowned Last Supper. Myself being a sort of natural writer, with a writer's automatic detachment and special perception of the situation at hand I jotted a few things down. Thought it might help with your education, which admittedly is going regrettably slowly. You, being a bit of a poet yourself, might appreciate some of the little flourishes I seem to have included. Speaking with all due modesty about my abilities, of course. Oh, uh, here my dear."

He handed it to her, smiling shyly.

★　　　★

★

Notes Observations and Humble
Wisdoms To Aid In Varia's Instruction Re
Important Stuff

†

I. There is one here tonight who, confidence un-streaked by small but rustforming leaks, zings in on whatever category of success he lusts for. Winner. Jaunty bursts of joie de vivre wreathe him. (remem to ask varia to guess who)

II. There is one here who sniffs and snuffles after a luring goal with the special urgency of malnutrition of spirit, and learns about mirages in the ultimate grasp at end. His hands, far from empty, hold a fool's tragedy.

III. There is one here who ties yellow balloons to each minute. O la.

IV. There is one here who keeps putting his hand on my leg.

V. There is one here who is breadpudding at the magician's meal—dull and thick and anaesthetized to his own bland lack. No blame. Painlack and luster-proof. Loll.

VI. There is one here who squints into his own eye and, blinkless, sees broken toys and bones and his own bloom trampled by toads, each toad bearing the seer's own fingerprints on its spideryclaw. All to dust but the eye, winkless. Iced eternal awareness, his curse.

&
MISCEL INFO & JOTS

—scampi tonight inferior
—name of hnd on leg st christopher—going
    thru chnges due to demotion—patience
—pregnant druid—obscene dancing—no
    class
—solomon very on tonight
—j christ pouting

65

—gd vint vino
—door priz as ALWAYZ to mary mag-
    dalene—rigged
—muzak nice
—baudelaire pedant but inform
—poe amuse all
—j joyce droll (remem tell varia his joke)

& &

QUESTIONS PUT TO AND ANSWERED BY BOARD

Questions:
  1. should we tell them crime pays?
  2. what'll we do about a new mythology?
  3. should we let them know processed food is
     intelligent life form?
  4. is the moon finally innocent?
  5. shall we allow perfect vending machines?
  6. are movie mags profound?
  7. should we allow paperclips to be produced
     mystically?
  8. what is yogurtism?
  9. shall we make wisdom hereditary?
 10. are children still depraved?
 11. is it time to withdraw the hoax of the Flavored
     Banana?
 12. should we tell them about the emperor's new
     clothes?
 13. are all rumors true?
 14. what'll we do about the americans?

Answers:
  1. they know.
  2. get the p.r. dept's ass in gear for one thing.
  3. you're kidding. is it?
  4. at last.

66

5. they exist now. we're test-marketing them secret-
    ly.
6. yes.
7. if possible. legal dept's working on patent
    problems.
8. yes.
9. no.
10. hopefully.
11. never.
12. what about them?
13. yes. we heard it through the grapevine.
14. hee hee.

& & &

In The Midst Of Salad It Was Mentioned That:
a) you cant always get what you want
b) there are gods and then there are gods
c) there is an unfilled need re alum siding

†

In The Midst Of Scampi And Hash Browns:
a) credulity quotients are generally low currently
b) we must do something amazing very soon

†

In The Thick Of Cherries Jubilee:
a) babies with ancient eyes deserve more
b) we must do this again soon (much clapping
    and waving of spoons)
c) life is just a bowl of ripened enigmas
d) the iroquois will be vindicated

Slowly, Varia rerolled the scroll and looked at Mouldie.

"You know, Mouldie, when I was a kid I always wished I was Harpo Marx. Now I know why."

•

As Mouldie tacked the scroll to the wall (and retacked it, again and again, he wanted it to be just right), Varia started the stove and made coffee, and wondered: these are the important secrets? Is this what I've been thirsting after? Even a hint of what I've been thirsting after?

"Your dress is torn." Mouldie said it without turning and with a tack in his mouth.
"I know. So what?" Varia had on a long white dress, filmy and dingy and torn.
"Mustn't let yourself go to pot, my curly curmudgeon. Next thing you know, you'll be scuffling around in sleazy slippers and watching daytime t.v. Hate to see a woman go to seed like that . . . Now. Your dream. Your girlish and dimply dream. Are you finally ready to tell me? Mustn't be shy; after all, among a few other things, I'm a goldstar dream analyst. I can extract significance—even glory—from your most trivial dream. Just hate to have to drag things out of you like this . . . "

He sat down, next to her at the table, and inched his chair closer to hers. Varia was trying to run her fingers through her hair, trying to unsnarl it, more a nervous gesture than a cosmetic one.
"Mouldie, have a sip of your coffee. Your breath defies description. . . . well, let's see, you and I were both in it, the dream, and so was Alex—"
"Forget him, child, he broke your fragile heart."
"Look, Mouldie, do you want to—"
"Yes."
"Well. The first part had a narrator—sort of a combination of Dick Lane—you know? The Roller Derby guy?"

"Roller what?"

"Never mind. Dick Lane and Andy Warhol, he's this artist, very big in New York for awhile—"

"I *know* that. Don't condescend to me, Varia."

"Oh shit. Look, he was talking into a mike—"

"A what?"

"A MICROPHONE."

"Go on."

"—like it was being taped, and, well, it started with me in bed, but awake. Oh, and the whole thing kept going back and forth in time—present and past tense. Well. So the narrator started talking . . .

NARRATOR: The air beside her bed is becoming denser. It's consolidating approximately at her shoulder, and the molecules are clumping and arranging themselves into what she senses to be a man-form. If she weren't paralyzed, she could turn over and look, but her entire nervous system has been removed cleverly: one neat incision at the top of her spine, an educated tug, and it was done . . .

(You were the doctor, Mouldie, so was Alex. You kept dissolving back and forth. And at this point, my boat turned into an operating theatre. Anyway . . .)

NARRATOR: The surgeon stood there, a red and white camiella, dangling the copper threads from his brilliant hand for the gallery to see . . . Listen to that applause!

DOCTOR: The nervous system can be removed as readily as varicose veins. How long did I take, Nurse?

NURSE: Twelve seconds exactly, Doctor.

DOCTOR: Well, there you are, Doctors! My theory has been proved beyond question, has it not? Twelve seconds of a neurosurgeon's time equals fifty dollars, five of these tricks per minute equals two-hundred-and-fifty big ones a minute, soooo imagine if you can, using the mathematical ability of an eight-year-old, the kind of income that can be yours if you join our hospital. Figure it out for yourselves.

NARRATOR: A rubbery left hand whips down the doctor's mask. Relegated now to scarfing the doctor's neck rakishly, the mask bobs about in artless bon vivant exuberance, in exact counterpoint to the body's movements.

DOCTOR: There's going to be an ever-increasing market for these humble-looking bunches of human threads . . . at this very moment, the transistor industry is crying out for an inexpensive, durable, adaptable means of transmitting signals—and what could possibly fill the bill more efficiently than this goodie I hold here, upraised before you?!

NARRATOR: Filled with zeal, aglow with enthusiasm, the doctor shakes the lumpen shreds above his head.

DOCTOR: Doctors! Fellow pioneers! I ask you—have you ever been offered an opportunity to equal this one I offer you today?

NARRATOR: The surgeon's arm pumps more eloquently, bits of nerve-endings fly off and stick to sterile surfaces. The nurse, yawning, flicks one off her right forearm.

DOCTOR: Join me, doctors! Follow me on the yellowbrick road of scientific progress! See your name in Popular Science! Be the guest-speaker at Kiwanis meetings!

NARRATOR: The surgeon's arm is involved in a weird dance of ecstasy, strands are whipping around his arm like a hundred malnourished octopi. They weave tentacles and caress his arm, a pumping porkchop. They are savoring the feast.

DOCTOR: Well doctors? How many of you are going to take that Big Step Forward today?!

NARRATOR: The man is now immobilized with Vision, rigid with Truth, except his arm, which is vibrating with such speed that it seems to be a pink fog attached to his right shoulder at a forty-five degree angle.

DOCTOR: Well, men?! Stand, doctors, stand up and be counted!!

NURSE: Doctor.

NARRATOR: It's Nurse Null, roused from lethargy.

DOCTOR: Yes, well, what is it, Sweetmeat? Are you ready to step forward? A loyal helpmate to these brave men of scio-technology?

NARRATOR: The surgeon's enflamed eyes challenge her with Ultimate Nursery, but do her eyes meet his in answer? No. They are fixed on his upraised but now motionless hand, which clutches a viscous dumpling with limp, short bristles noodling from his fist. Delicate spaghettini decorates the operating theatre, the law of centrifugal force now bowing to the law of gravity. One by one, the shreds shrivel and fall from the walls and attendants.

NURSE: Doctor Earnesto, you've just ruined the advertising sample.

(Then I'm back in bed, here, in the boat, still paralyzed, and you, Mouldie, you're standing by the bed but you look like, well frankly, sort of a pile of gnarls and bones. I can't move, but I try to speak:)

> —Who. Who's there. Where you. Who?
> —Just me. Just Mouldie. Old M.
> —How? How?

—Well, easy door, really, squeezed through the *o* in Earnesto.

—Ah, all's well, through the *o,* o ho, of course. Old Mouldie, ah.

—I've brought your nerves back, repaired and total. Possible because you didn't sign an operating contract. Lucky or wise, don't know which of you. Matters, of course, ponder it, one of these down days you'll give them license to destroy you, and then old Mouldie won't help. Can't then. Nonetheless and howsomever, keep your rights in your constant pocket.

(Then you evaporated, and I seemed to be suddenly . . . acting, you know? In a film. Only I was also describing my own thoughts and actions out loud, like a narrator of myself. But all in one person. I also seemed very stoned and melodramatic. Well. I got out of bed slowly and said:)

—No time for sleep, this. Time for tea and the company of candleflame. I must consider my shambling friend and his remarkable cure of my sudden paralysis. I must reform his words in the tallow candleglow so that I might brand them on my voice and understand them better. I must slowly wind his words through the candle's flame to see their true shade, knowing in advance the result will be: white. Always white. I must light a candle to insure privacy for a few minutes . . . when this boat absorbs the night, the busy beings of a thousand epochs wend their way through here, regardless of my need for solitude. By morning the air in here is worn thin by the trample of roman chariots, flapper dancers, lost children of medieval wars, stockbrokers

in morning coats and tickertape chains of
questionmarks, dwarves in angeldrag, mothers
suffocated by rejections, popes and their mute
mistresses, bald and toothless spoils of just
crusades, Shirley Temple dimpletons, circus
acrobats grown rich with wise investments in
real estate, recent suburban housewives con-
demned to boredom and mirrors, alcoholic
grandfather clocks, suicidal lemmings, trea-
sonous doorknobs, and an occasional camp
follower of laser theorists' conventions.

I wend my way through the crowd and
eventually reach the table.
Matches. Shit. Where did I . . . where's
the . . . here. Okay. Light. Now stoke fire.
Tea, camomile . . .
A common occurrence is happening: I find
myself ten minutes ahead of the present, and
can watch it with the detachment and analy-
tical clearness of retrospect. Having cleared
the room with light, and started the tea, and
brushed my hair in the window reflection, I
sat at the table and started to unreel Mouldie's
words in the flame. Almost immediately the
words broke into syllables, added a third
dimension, lumped themselves into a rough
but recognizable likeness of my friend, then
blended perfectly.
Mouldie, you rattling heap. I really need to be
alone. I got an extra cup down from the
jumbled shelf. This was going to be a long
night, and Mouldie saw through my feeble
protest. His face shuffled various smiles, and
settled for a rueful one.
—What's wit alone, lady? What's wit tink?

73

Why you not understan tings firs' time round?
—I studied him. The wisdom of this visual
disaster. Idiot savant. Physical debris dump.
Guru. Snob. Mouldie, reflection hardly equals
stupidity. And why do *you* affect oral il-
literacy?

A slow Mouldie headnod.

—Lissen kid, dere's tings for you to know and
not know. When you get whar I'm at, den you
got time to be a smartass.

—Mouldie continued, slipping easily back
into perfect middleclass english, but flavored
with german accent, vicinity of Düsseldorf.

—I believe you received a greeting card last
christmas holiday?

—Mmm. Yes. From the health inspector.
Gave it to me with the notice-to-abate-
nuisance-order the week before christmas. I
remember he flushed with shyness and good-
will as he nailed the card and destruction
notice together to my door. I found the
contrast charming. Why?

—Find it, please.

—Well, I'll look. You pour the tea, alright?
Where does one begin looking for a two-
month-lost christmas card? I decided to use
the onion strategy: starting from the center,
then making concentric circles, or actually, a
spiral, til the object, i.e., card, was found.
Mouldie nodded approval, noticing my technique. Mouldie poured tea. Mouldie counted
camomile flowertops rehydrating in the pot.
Mouldie reheated the tea without comment
when it cooled. Mouldie continued to admire
my technique. Mouldie threw out reheated
and recooled tea. Mouldie nodded encourage-
ment. Mouldie made new tea. Mouldie took a

short nap. Mouldie reheated tea. Mouldie
nodded at me encouragingly.
—I found it!

(Suddenly the scene dissolves into a newspaper headline, like
a 1940 movie, you know, Mouldie?"
"Go on."
"Well, it read—)

BAROQUE CHRISTMAS CARD DIS-
LODGED FROM BETWEEN FEATHER-
STACK AND COMPOST BARREL
complete story on pg I part III

So the pages turn in a flurry, and . . .)

An embossed bit of rococo paperpulp has
been uncovered in a recent archeological dig,
the instigators and participants of which are
considered by recognized experts to be ill-
trained, unprofessional, and outside the main-
stream of organized thought.
The behavior of the digging party has been
censored and deplored by E. (Skim) Cerfis,
Grand Marshal of ADAPT (American Digging And Probing Tong) as being 'amateurish,
bizarre, and without redeeming social significance'. Furthermore, the leading figure in this
unauthorized expedition has been found by a
federal court to be guilty as charged on the
following counts:
  1) improper procedure through life
  2) molestation of high ideals
  3) inability to relate meaningfully to society
  4) ratty and weird clothes

(Now the ann—uh, Mouldie, are you following this alright?"
"O sure."
"The Andy Warhol-Roller Derby guy, the narrator, is back.

75

The camera's on him, the newspaper's disappeared . . .)

NARRATOR: In a spontaneous transmedia search for truth, we absolve the above newspaper clipping of all pertinence, and, fickle parasites lost in coy sucking, we attach outselves to a relatively flamboyant television camera, imbedded in the courtroom. Whrr. See the big black camera. Hear it whrr. See the big black camera edit instinctively. See the hand-held sponge soak up an event. See the big black camera go. Go camera go. See what comes out of the camera. Whrr.

Camera pans courtroom.

Lining the regulation benches of the spectator section are retired vultures and broken bridge clubs, in placid wait. Hush. Center aisle gleams around shoe-scruffs. Camera slides without comment to the jury box: freshly opened carton of eggs. Nary a crack. In television makeup, in unison, they turn their best oval profiles to the lens. Big black box goes whrr and on to the court recorder. He, known as C. R. even to his intimates, is a suspected catatonic. Balding. Glazed. Only his hands are saved from stasis. They flutter ceaselessly in silent taps. The lens discounts him and swivels on to the prosecutor . . .

(Do you think he symbolized Alex, too, Mouldie?"
"Forget him, child, he broke your fra—"
"Never mind.)

NARRATOR: Lancelot Wolverine; conservative chic; creased beige over all; no distinguishing scars; most notable characteristic: chalkdust on right thumb and forefinger, renewed daily by drawing the line to be stepped over by God in his sometimes muddled search for the right side to be on. Rubbing his fingers together, L.W. allows his eye to follow the camera's sweep to the defendant, who is seated at the table of the defense. A medusa in tatters.

(That's me, of course."
"You tell it, I'll analyze it.")

NARRATOR: She has silently refused to stand for sentencing, as just moments ago, she silently refused to stand for the jury's verdict. She is motionless, except for her eyes, which are focused on an invisible canvas four feet in front of her. Impatient and quick, her eyebeams sketch in a Norman Rockwell hometown-justice scene. Hmmn. Not bad. With an even surer stroke, her eyes speed in the colors and then details. Satisfied, she begins the forged signature just as the judge stands to deliver sentence. We notice that he's entirely covered with a black sack. Or is it just that he's a genuine void? Either way, each observer should fill the allotted space in his t.v. screen with a reasonably clear picture (drawing or photo) of his favorite private judge. The timehonored cut-and-paste method is recommended. Safety scissors with rounded tips, please.
Sshh. Quiet now, the judge speaks.

JUDGE: The accused, having been tried and found guilty of, well, having been tried and found guilty by twelve of her peers, will please remain standing to receive the sentence of the court.

NARRATOR: The defendant remains seated. The judge ignores it. The judge continues.

JUDGE: The sentence is . . . envelope, please, usherette.

NARRATOR: An unmarked door at the side of the courtroom opens, and there appears a bunnytwitch glowgirl who sidles and swarms up to the podium. Three-quarter view, tits awing, ambition aswing on a haunch. She extends her arm in phallic challenge to judge and homeviewers alike. The judge, in timeless rutdance, snatches the envelope with his polished if invisible left hand, while his right demurely positions yellow legalsize

77

notepad over his appointed but equally invisible private parts.

JUDGE: Thank you, Miss X, for escorting the envelope from the sealed vault. And . . . now . . . members of the academy and folks at home, the sentence you've all been waiting—

NARRATOR: Suddenly the accused, convicted, and about to be sentenced prisoner bolts up with the grace of the enlightened, fumbles with her skirt, plunges her hand into the mysteries of her naval, searches for and seizes a tiny but steadily enlarging object, dashes from the table of her own trusted but absent defense counsel to the sacrosanct podium and flagrantly attacks judge and usherette alike with the now fullgrown can of what—although cleverly labeled MACE—proves itself to be the lethal raspberryflavored d.d.t.based Keep Your Shady Parts Dainty Lady vaginal spray.

Instantly numbed, the victims fall instinctively into an unrehearsed but inspired routine that was based on an idea sent in by a homemaker from Des Moines, Iowa, a Mrs. Janie Doright, who at this very minute is frolicking with husband Ernie on the private beach of the MotelSleepTite, located in the heart of the playground of the stars, Long Beach, California! Congratulations Mrs. Doright for having this week's winning idea! And now, fellas and gals, while Mrs. D. and her hubby relax on their all-expense-paid vacation and enjoy their free bonus case of our sponsor's product, we're going to let you see for yourself a dramatic simulation of Mrs. Doright's idea . . .

. . . watch carefully now and see both a distinguished judge and an aspiring usherette demonstrate a time-lapse rhapsody of benumbment becoming rigidity becoming decomposition becoming molecular rearrangement becoming—becoming—lo! Where once was a presumably middleaged judge, now evolves a compost barrel! What you knew to be a silver-screen debutante has metamorphosed into a final featherstack! The can-holding hand lurches along with them in time-lapse rhythm and participates in the drama in its own small way: the grasping fingers now hold not a misleadingly labeled aerosol can, but an embossed bit of rococo paperpulp, a baroque christmas card!!

(You see, you and I, we're back on the boat again, and I'm handing you the christmas card. You seem pleased that I finally found it, and I'm still stoned and narrating my own behavior. I think that's significant, that *I'm* my own narrator . . . uh, well, then you say—)

—Aha. Bien, Donnez-moi, le, la, whatchit, card. Here. Place el cardo sur la table avec godspeed. Zip.
—I do as directed.
—Dat's a good girl. Sit. Watch.
—We are the prototype of all teams, a skeleton crew of any action force, the born commander and his willing robot. I sit. I watch. I try to imagine a two-year-old Mouldie, yellowcurled and new, dabbling through an idyllic poppyfield, learning ladybugs and locomotion. I try. I try again. One more time. A picture finally surfaces . . . a foetal Mouldie, translucent with incompletion, burbling piglatin opinions into prenatal fluids. Why must sentiment die repeated horrible deaths? Why couldn't Truth have chosen a horseshoe instead of a circle? If the Circular Cosmic Hypostasis could be pried open, even a little, just think! A christmas morning of loose ends! A universe of floating propositions!

79

—You're not watching.

—A wobbling glare from Mouldie. I see that he has propped the card against the candlestem.

—Observe pay if attention you will my what little happens next pear.

—Don't be tedious, Mouldie. I refuse to unravel your braided sentences.

—Don't play dumb. That one was easy.

—It's the principle. Do it yourself.

—A flaccid mind courts disaster, and I fear you are approaching the dull dumpling stage . . . I SAID, pay attention my little pear; observe if you will what happens next.

—Aha! you added a semicolon. No wonder. You could be disqualified for that.

—Wrong. It was at the end, first time around.

—That's a lie, Mouldie.

—No, that's a subtlety that was lost on you. I even gave you a hint, a clue . . . *pay attention* was tucked in there, if you'll recall.

—You've sucked me into this game for the last time, I swear it.

—What's wit game, lady?

—Look, you glob of verbal tricks—Oh, that's cute, Mouldie, that's just a dynamite hat.

—Mouldie has wandered into a napoleonic moment, and has assumed a three-cornered hat and partially buttoned coat.

A suggestion of garlic drifts in, and French peasants gather ominously outside the door. Mouldie sips his bordeaux.

O Jesus, I'm losing sleep over this? Mouldie, sensitive to a fault, immediately puts his toys away, hesitating only over the bordeaux.

—REGARDE! Tu ne dois pas screw around no more. Lookee.

—He levels his crooked finger at the christmas
card. The card is six inches square, embossed
so heavily that it's nearly a bas relief. In the
center is a feeding trough, ornately carved and
painted. In the· trough is impossible hay,
glowing and curving over the edge. In the hay
is the inevitable but appealing christchild, his
hands joined in prayer. Above his head a gold
oval hovers. The trough, hay, baby, and oval
are enclosed within a wreath of what appears
to be gold and silver wires, painstakingly
twisted into elaborate leaves, tendrils, berries,
flowers, branches, acorns, pinecorns, bows,
half-hitch release knots, prize-winning original
embroidery stitches, morning glory vines, bag-
gywrinkles, tangled kitestring, thin rolled
strips of tin from the tops of sardine cans,
stylized signs of the zodiac, several six-
pointed stars, and one obscure but distinguish-
able cross.

A small streak mars the lower lefthand corner
of the card, probably where it had touched the
compost barrel. Candleflare flickers the intricacies of design into movement . . . minor
jumps and starts, like small springs unwinding
from themselves. Colors are ancient shades of
traditional joy. Peace. Innocence dancing to
the silent tune of candleblow. Christe eleison,
little god in brocade rags.

Looks quite content, he does, happy under his
spinning halo, secure within his wreath. Wire
womb, mass-produced and hung on door-
hooks yearly, in exact season . . . all those
polished front doors vaguely hoping that the
wreath-hole will fill itself somehow with a
hay-borne godbaby. Sometime . . . Doors

opened daily to another disappointment. Time gone, new year, wreaths closeted for another year, dust, rust. Must it be a god the hole accepts? If I were to perch there, in one of a million holiday vacuums, would I be ousted? Would anyone notice that my fingerprints were wrong? My credentials not in order, in fact, nonexistent? My halo, a bogus wire, crimped unconvincingly if you looked closely? Would I incur the wrath of the world if I filled a hole reserved for someone who has a surplus of reserved holes? So many holes, he could never get around to each one, even for a second, even if he wanted to? And would he mind if some disgruntled hole-owner went to the top and informed him that a disheveled creature was testing squatter's rights in his reserved space?

On this card he looks kind. Mellow. Relaxed. A little resigned maybe. The perpetual sigh of wisdom? Is he thinking of all those wreaths, all those hopes?

The candle winkles lower. It looks like his hands moved. They did, his hands are moving—grasping the trough-edge. A divine foot appears. A fancy ragged bummy pudges itself up and over. A bounce down, dipsy, knees a bit bent, hands out for balance. Sway. He toddles to the edge of the wreath . . . casts about for a place to cross. The wreath, being about two inches wide at every point, is no easy obstacle for him to hurdle safely.

He carefully picks his way over: a foothold on a french knot here, a grasp on an acorn there, a baggywrinkle gives way under a heel, ah, better, a cancercrab's sturdy back, watch that

star to your left, oops did you see that, a pinecone almost pricked his hand, no, no, not there, grab that curvy thing—
caught up in maneuvers, Mouldie and I can't avoid giving advice—
You're almost there, watch the tangles, aha! Well done! A first foot, then a second, onto the table. One hand raised in salutation or victory, one hand on a tangle, balancing: dimply godkin, he steadies himself for a moment—
caught up in meaningful experience, Mouldie and I can't avoid staring—
then he tom thumbs his way over to Mouldie's now-empty wine glass. He stands there, dabbling his toe in a spilled drop of wine, and glances at Mouldie expectantly.
Mouldie offers his finger. The little one clambers on. Mouldie smoothly raises his precious finger-rider to the rim and carefully helps him into the bowl of the glass. The child settles into a plump lotus—
caught up in his charisma, Mouldie and I can't avoid
         THE INCANDESCENT INFANT
. . . who says:
—I am the child you called mantra. I am the child you probed for gold. I am the child you poised on a coin, that wears your eyes rehearsed in aversion while your hands search my smile. But my smile fails you in its perfection: for where are the breathing shadows you need to fold into? They are there, there, behind me, and in them are riddles, riddles and pains, webs too: many webs with infinite spiders leering, winking. But I am Ernie with a million dancing shadows. Above

them all, my toes fly over mountains and sense and skin. Patterns dissolve beneath my spin. Behind my eyes of spangle and salt—salt of a dozen colors—I am just god with a million ernie shadows. And in them you must prance to the end of pain. In them you must sing anthems that never end and never repeat. In them you must find me with eyes and toes and groins. Remember: I float through sticky tunnels, leaving anthems hung like moss for spiders and song-eaters. I will feed the webs with breath as I shine through, I, Ernie!

•

Well, that's it." Varia looked at Mouldie expectantly. Mouldie nodded, deep in thought, then asked, "Who's Harpo Marx?"

• • •

Varia lit a cigarette and stared at the empty chair where Mouldie had been. Then, mechanically, she reached across the table for a bottle of brandy, uncorked it, and poured into her coffee . . .
The stone Mouldie had brought for her was on the table—she picked it up . . . "teaching aid—" then going to the sink, she dropped it into a glass of water to soak clean.
She watched the stone soak. Then she glanced over to the wall behind her and looked at the scroll; she watched it hang. She walked to the table, lit another cigarette from the one she was just finishing, put more coal in the stove, ignoring the piece that fell on the floor, turned back to the table, drank half the cup of brandied coffee, went over to the scroll and

began to read it again. As she read she wondered, Is this—gibberish—all Mouldie can teach me? Is this IT? Or am I being stupid? What if the true essence of wisdom is soaking in my sink and hanging on my wall . . . Is this what they always tried to get me to listen to? . . . What my own great-great-grandmother was trying to teach me?

She smoked and leaned back against the high bed that was behind her; one hand held a cigarette, one hand untangled the chaos that was her hair. She stared at the scroll as her mind raced away from it:

Is *this* what Grandmère tried to whisper to me on her deathbed? Is this what her final gargle spelled out? Or did she know more? Did the fact that she was fullblooded Iroquois give her some pure depth, some certain pride, missing in me, a mongrel?

Did she cry over her children and her children's children with their passionate if careless mixing of blood? How did she really feel about her French son-in-law, not to mention her pushy Irish grandson-in-law? Did she mind scrubbing office floors all those years? Or did she discover a timeless rhythm with her sponge? Did she chant in time? Could she have reached euphoria night after scrubbing night? And here we all felt sorry for her . . . She may well have been a floorwax junkie, hooked on the ritual. Slop whoosh. Slop whoosh. Secret nirvana. Except of course on Saturday night, which she always had off . . . No matter what, Grandmère—funny how we all called her that, regardless of our exact relationship to her, well, not counting her third son who always referred to her as That Indian Lady . . . he was never comfortable with his heritage, which is probably why he made a career of the navy—would always insist on having Saturday nights off. Even in her oldest age, she'd mumble about a girl needing one night a week to just plain boogie. Well.

I wonder if she missed the floors when she stopped. Maybe if it hadn't happened so suddenly. It seemed so weird—one day

Grandmère's a floorscrubber, the next day she's making a fucking fortune doing t.v. commercials. Iroquois became so stylish so . . . abruptly . . . she never really had time to get used to the money, the fame, having people—even Germans—stop her on the street for her autograph. Just didn't have time . . . swallowed her up, it did: There goes, went, one grand old Indian dame, gobbled by Hollywood. But then for all I know, she was sneaking floors in at night, after staggering out of Cyrano's at two. God, how she used to embarrass me, those sunglasses, that muttering, chants I suppose, in the back seat of her Rolls, having the chauffeur drop her off in front of obscure office buildings on side streets, off the Miracle Mile . . . I couldn't bear to witness it.

Well, I was young. Everything is embarrassing when you're that young. The way she used to cackle, actually a very classic cackle, like an imitation of an old Indian squaw doing a cackle, I used to just die. Heukl, heukl, heukl, Varia, I tell you child, heukl heukl, if your poor old dead great-great-grandpapa could see me now! Stop the car Morris, I want to check out the Tishman building, no—wait—heukl forget it, I've got an early makeup call tomorrow, heukl wheeze DRIVE ON.

I think she always secretly enjoyed the fact that my great-great-grandfather was a Jesuit missionary in Canada. In fact, she probably did it for the shock value: Sorry, Leaping Bear, I'm not going to marry you after all, well, what can I tell you . . . It's the Jesuit, yes I know, but I can't help myself . . . I'd rather be his back-street girl than your squaw, if we're gonna call a spade a spade. Well let them talk. Love conquers all, we'll make it work.

So he, Grandpère, knocked the horny little Indian maid up when she was fifteen, in the vestibule of the little log chapel, family legend has it. And then, let's see, when she was sixteen, then when she was eighteen-and-a-half, again when she was

86

nineteen— and so on through three daughters and four sons. None of her children or her children's children or her children's children's children asked her about what she had learned in the village of her youth—I know that because she used to comment on it all the time:
'Don't any of you halfbreeds want to know the secrets of your ancestors? Hmmn? Go on, ask me, ask me anything. I can tell you. Well? No? So stay dumb. Who cares?'
I never asked her, not because I wanted to stay dumb, but because I didn't believe a word she said anyway. And besides that, I didn't want to be the only one in the family who could be cornered by the crazy old grandmother with her tales of Indian lore. It was a family status symbol: if you had any cool at all, you could avoid Grandmère.

Only when she was on her deathbed, when she gargled and hissed and spattered at me with a kind of manic urgency, did I start to take her seriously. I realized then, too late, of course, that she wouldn't be going to all that trouble, and exerting her last bit of earthly strength, just to jive me.

Grandmère, will you ever forgive me my cynicism? Will you tell me now what you tried without luck to spit at me then, on your telegram-laden deathbed? Will you whisper across a plane or two of existence? Will you ride the crest of a time warp, the eternal withered surfer, hanging ten as you cut across to your desperate great-great-granddaughter?
Will you teach me the secret rhythms of a sponge? Can I reach into the sacred bucket, tin I think, where you sloshed your mysteries?
Grandmère, I know nothing of anything. I understand nothing. I know only that I was mistaken about all the things I thought I knew. Grandmère, can you help me smoke less?
Grandmère, Iroquois Saint, Revered Ancestress, Seed of our Mongrel Dynasty, Drill Instructor of our shamefully suburban family, Our Brown Lady Who Claimed Seven Immaculate Conceptions, Main Mistress of a Jesuit, Heathen

Victim of a Missionary, Coldhearted Rejector of a Dear-Johned Brave, Holy Primitive Superstar, Certain Groomer of Office Linoleum, Abused Elder of Unimaginative Offspring: help me cope.

Help me be sure of anything. My name, I'm not even sure of my name; is it *really* Varia, or is actually Thalia or Mary Jo or Mona and what if, for their own perverse reasons, my parents, your great-grandson and his wife, what if they've fooled me all these years? I don't know if they did that, but if they did, I don't know why they did it.

You see?

I am now innocent of conclusions. I have stumbled this far on a road of intellectual banana peels. It's ruined my nerves. It's given me deep circles under my eyes. It's made me chain-smoke. It hasn't totally ruined my hair or figure yet thank god.

But who knows? Grandmère, it's made me so frantic that I snap at Mouldie, the only hope I seem to have. For that matter, it's made me frantic enough to admit Mouldie exists, to talk to him, to listen to him. *That's* the issue, not my snapping at him.

Grandmère, you knew me before, you knew me until you died. Did you see the shadow of this day, is that what you were trying so hard to sputter at me? Were you trying to save me from these psychic tatters? Did you, in your last spasm of wisdom, know that soon I was to know that I didn't know anything? Were you trying to give me some little shred of timeless legend, some secret word to hang onto at times like this?

A key.

Were you trying to give me a key of some kind? Grandmère, do you see this scroll that Mouldie so carefully prepared for me? Can you do better? Grandmère, I've tried nearly everything: I've ransacked Herman Hesse. I read The Prophet when I was sure no-one was looking. I've read Dear Abby twice, I can't describe how low I was. I've consulted madmen. I went to a luncheon, where there were only women in girdles

and corsages. I went to a feminist meeting, where there were only women in anger. I went to a seance. I went to a circus, and was sure I was close to the heart of the matter. I've gone from city to city, from canyon to beach, from desert to bay. I bleached my hair once.
Nothing.
I've listened to salesgirls whisper together. Their giggles sounded so definite. I've begged hi-way patrolmen to tell me all they know. I've gone from bed to bed in my search. From fourposter to waterbed to sleeping bag. I've gone from men to boys to old men with pinky rings.
I sharpened my questions on their shoulder blades. My tape recorder kept track of all they said in their sleep. They lied, so often lied or were mistaken. I honed my wonder on their orgasms.
I payed such close attention to their coming.
I planted questionmarks in their hair, I learned cunning watching them shave.
I perfected my smile on their gloriously furred bellies. I learned to explode ecstatically and harmlessly. They taught my thighs to hum. They taught my hands to dance like Isadora Duncan. They taught my hair to wisp over their collective face. They taught my breasts to stand at attention. They taught me to feed them breakfast. The old men taught me the terrors of growing old with nothing but your body. The boys taught me once again the horrors of adolescence. The young men schooled me in their loneliness and needs. They rehearsed their fantasies on me. They taught me to love them forever, in spite of their fantasies. They taught me to lean towards them like a sailboat into the wind. They taught my name to trail after them like the tail of a kite. They trapped my fingers in their hair and their mouths. They trapped me like a moth in a web of touches and unknowns. They pinned me like a butterfly in the steady rhythm of their loins. Each thrust drove me deeper into their debt.
They taught me the ultimate mysteries of gooseflesh. They taught me superior muscle control. They taught me to respect

buttocks. They taught my body to sing softly when they reached for me in their sleep.

They taught me a hell of a lot, didn't they?

Ah, but Grandmère, they didn't teach me what I knew I had to know. Grandmère, wise if dead old great-great-grandmother, if this rotten scroll is the best Mouldie can do, surely you can do better?

If the aforementioned is all that men can do, surely you can add a little something.

If my sitting here on this godforsaken houseboat for three months is a worthwhile discipline, surely you'll send me a sign? Grandmere, do you know what they're saying?

You'd better listen, since it reflects on you, you know.

They're saying I'm disintegrating.

Benny wrote me from New York, he said that's what my good friends in New York are saying. Alex is in L.A. now, he had his agent write to me and he said that in L.A., they say I'm stark raving mad. No word from London and I'm sure it's just as well.

Am I?

Are they right?

I admit I know nothing, but does it make me mad to be trying to find out something? Anything? Does it make me mad to admit there are important secrets?

Grandmère, the existence of the secrets is ruining my life. They've caused me to suspect streetlights, to accuse gas stations, to fear markets. They've led me like sirens to this bloody hole in the wall of a boat. Grandmère, these important secrets are like terrible membranes between all the different layers of my life. My life's become a horribly imbalanced club sandwich.

The best I can do at the moment is try to stack things up, helter-skelter you might say, just work like mad to keep the layers one on top the other, screw order, I don't care *what* order they're in, just—if I can keep any one layer, or god forbid, all of the whole mess, from sliding off the tray onto the floor in a gooey mayonnaise-ridden disaster.

Grandmère, do you see the enormity of this? Are you aware of how many people, regular people you and I know, willingly let one or more layers fall off? The membrane of secrets is usually the first to go. Can you bear it? But on the other hand, could they be right? Is it perhaps too much to expect to stagger through life with the whole sandwich? Why? I want it. As long as the whole sandwich exists, why can't I have it all? Why should I jettison part of MY sandwich?

Grandmère, give me a ray of hope. A hint. Should I, would it be better in the long run, to let one layer skid off? If so, how about gas stations and dandruff? T.v. ads. Checking accounts, carwashes. Let's face it, I've just about lost that layer as it is. Laughter and tears I refuse to give up, dreams, no, druid legends, no, unknown secrets, never, making love, forget it.

You see? What choice is there? Gas stations are all I can spare, and for that matter, I can't go back to anywhere if I lose that layer completely.

Grandmère, don't desert me now, in this my blackest hour.

●　　●　　●

"Telegram for you, my dear."

Varia jumped, dropping the long ash from her cigarette.

"What? Oh, Mouldie, Christ, you . . . I was thinking."

"Yes, yes, I know you were my dear, which is why I busied myself polishing the brass fittings here and uh, there on the boat, to keep out of your hair, you see, while you were thinking that is, just thought I'd do a little voluntary menial labor to impress upon you my good intentions and—no! Don't thank me! I didn't do it for thanks or kudos, don'tcha know, kudos I never lust after my dear, just did it to keep out of your hair. They do look all nice and glowy though, don't they? The fittings, that is.

Also I paced around the edge of the roof twelve times, just to keep fit. You might do the same, buttercup, be good for you. A deep kneebend or two would be excellent too, I might add. Upper thighs."

"The telegram—?"

"Ah, yes! Came slipping and sliding right under the door you know . . . just a split-second after I came in, and when I peeked out the porthole, not a living soul was there. Strange and mystical. Well, I suppose you want to open it, don't you?"

"Right." Varia tore open the envelope.

"Wait a minute. This isn't a telegram, it's a formletter printed to *look* like a telegram."

DEAR SIR OR MADAM:
VERY SORRY I CANNOT GIVE PER-
SONAL REPLY TO ALL INQUIRIES RE
MY RISE TO FAME IN HOLLYWOOD
STOP THANK YOU FOR YOUR IN-
TEREST HOWEVER STOP THE BEST OF
LUCK TO YOU STOP
    FLOPPING DOVE COUTURE
    IROQUOIS COMMERCIAL
    QUEEN

•

Telegram, formletter, still in hand, Varia went to the door and looked out the leaded glass window set in it. She ran an index finger over one eyebrow, again and again.

Snowing. And I didn't even notice. Wonder how long

it's . . . been snowing. Was it snowing when I got up? Was it
snowing all night last night? Will it go on forever? There's
something so perverse about snow on water . . . unnatural.
Unnatural snow. Unnatural relationship, snow meeting
water. Shocking. Futile. Futile as a formletter from the
dead . . . makes about as much sense, too. Jesus, I must—
there must be . . .
My name is Varia.
No, no, I AM Varia. This is a china cup. It's in my hand. My
left hand. It has a small chip. The cup. There's coffee in it.
Steaming. I made the coffee on the stove into which I put the
coal earlier.
Well, okay so far.
I am Varia and everything's going to be alright. It's snowing,
it's February, no, shit, it's January, I hate it when I do
that . . . It's January and the boat's creaking. I have rings
on all of my fingers except one. And my thumbs, never rings
on thumbs.

Snow makes the water so flat. Weird. Two dimensional. Seen
through a gauze. The gauze is three dimensional though,
which is even weirder (there once was a girl who had a curl
right in the middle of her forehead and when she was good
she was very very good and when she was bad she was
horrid).
Bad she was horrid. Christ. Early schizophrenic program-
ming if I ever . . . three-year-olds bearing the weight of
monkey-demons. How do we survive? *Do* we . . .
Grandmère, there's nothing funny about a rejection slip.
Slammed doors, closed windows, pockets of silence. A huge
ghostly rubber stamp screaming WRONG, emblazoned on
brick walls at the end of dead-end streets. In such innocence
we wander. In such dumb.

What's Varia doing now? She's on this strange boat in the
middle of the endless snowstorm. Well, of course. What else
would she be doing?

93

How about collecting rejection slips from the dead. Could she be doing that instead? She might be, but who knows, the two aren't mutually exclusive. She might be collecting rejection slips from the dead on a houseboat during the endless snowstorm. On the other hand, she might be a dead rejection slip connected to a snowstorm enduring an endless houseboat.

Or she might be a snowboat rejecting an endless stormhouse.

Or she might be the endsnow housing a rejected boatstorm. Or she might simply be your basic imploding gold filigree watchlob.

Who's to say.

Grandmère is apparently not going to say. Flopping Dove Couture Ave., not a thru-street, all innocent wanderers of Ultimate Dumb welcome.

Maybe that's the point. Maybe it's a great worn wheel, with a million spokes, each spoke having a definite length . . . hopeless ants, we crawl up each spoke, turn around, hit the hub again, try another spoke, another dead-end spoke, back again, check in with the hub, up-down another spoke, hurry time's running out, got to get all the spokes covered, you can see how important it is, don't miss a spoke. Hi hub, gasp, another spoke, o I'm doing it, I'm covering millions of spokes, each dead-end spokestreet crossed off the list one after the other, say, this is Important Business, got to cover them all so I can get back to the hub which is where I started.

And the Forever Snow covers the tracks so it looks like virgin territory to the next earnest ant. What happens to the ones who don't make it back to the hub? What if you just stay, sort of make camp and settle in, on one spoke or another? Well, that's common enough I suppose . . . but how about a third choice, how about if the ant figures out how to fly at the end of a spoke, turns into a flying termite. Whatever. Flies away. The hell with the wheel, see what else is going on out there.

How many layers of the psychic club sandwich would be discarded and left on the wheel? How many can a termite carry and deal with effectively? How many dead-end spoke-streets are repositories for decomposing sandwich sections? Why hasn't the Gallup Poll looked into this? For a world that bows and scrapes to the golden calf of percentages and ratios, why has this been overlooked?

Is this subversive? Am I subversive?

Are we back to another dreary case of the emperor's new clothes? Is there a consensus, unspoken of course, that we won't discuss the issue of decomposing sandwich parts? Shall we all pretend the world's an automat of spunky new sandwiches? Is garbage collection only acceptable on a material level? Or are psychiatrists ego-garbage collectors? Are priests soul-garbage collectors? Are husbands and wives love-garbage collectors? Are children guilt-garbage collectors? If so, if even maybe so, then it does seem that the men in the grey trucks at dawn, rattling their lids, are the only real successes in the field.

Is it all a system of failure? Is that what they were teaching in the philosophy classes I cut so long ago? While I was out being young and irresponsible, is that what I was missing? Did I miss a litany of negation that I might have learned, that might have saved me this trouble? Were they all hunched over in their dusty rooms, gathered in a camaraderie of common knowledge, chanting in low hypnotized tones? What were they learning to say?

While I was humming on a beach, popping seaweed bladders, or getting drunk with the lowlife Mother warned me against, what were they learning to say?

Is it too late for me? Do I know too much and too little to learn the litany now? Is my final punishment for cutting class a cracked coffeecup in an endless snowstorm?

Is that tacky formletter from Grandmère what they cursed me with when they whispered and rustled about, saying I had rather disappointed their expectations—after all, they had hoped I'd be a bright light in their school, not a drunk sex-crazed ne'er-do-well: How can you do this to yourself, child, we're so concerned, how can you go in *two years* from poetry awards to *this?* Would you like to have a conference with the chaplain? He's always been so fon—alright, Missy, wipe that smirk off your face. You are in no position . . . We know you're bright enough. You're under*achieving,* Varia, you're capable of so much more. (Mother Superior paused here, thoughtful and sighing.) Well, my dear, you've mocked us with your attitude and behavior, you've ignored the seriousness of probation, so we have no alternative now. We must . . . ask you to leave. After all, you won't even let us *try* to help you. You've become . . . Intractable. God help you, child, it's true. You're just wasting your parents' hardearned money—

Now wait, Sister, my father is to money what St. Francis was to birds and rodents, I mean money just sort of *heels*—

I'm sorry, my dear, we had expected great things of you. And, well, look at you.

They couldn't understand that I needed to gather the wisdoms of tattooed winos.

They didn't understand that I needed to learn the litany of seaweed at the same time they were teaching other psalms in philosophy class. Did there have to be a choice? Was there a choice? Did a choice make me?

I choose to be me. I am Varia, with a cup in my hand. Snow falls. The boat rolls in a pleasant minor way. Snow falls. Coals glow through the antique iron stove grill. Glimmer. Windows steam. Coffee-smell is everywhere. Snow falls. Silence screams at me: Listen, the snow's falling.

•　　•　　•

Varia walked away from the door and around the small

room. Her body was fluid, but her legs stiff . . . she grazed surfaces, she floated jerkily. Caged and lost, it was all wrong, no place to rest, to alight. Bird with no place to land, hopeless. She twisted the telegram into a stiff strand. She forgot the coffee; the pot sizzled dry. A wall-hung mirror hooked into her scanning glance.

I wonder if I get seven years good luck for repairing a mirror that someone else broke. I should, flip side of the coin and all. Those gullfeathers look good around it . . . featherframed fixed mirror. Could be worse. Could be pink plastic with bas-relief roses and a price sticker that never quite comes off. The glue, the glue never really leaves. They must do that on purpose, just so you never forget you bought it. On the other hand, if you stole a mirror from a dime store, and couldn't get all the glue off, it'd be a whole different statement: accusatory gluemark pointing at you whenever you looked. They get you either way (there once was a girl who had a curl right in the middle).

There once was a mirror who had a girl right in the middle. Using the term *girl* loosely . . . god. Mouldie was right. I look savaged. What did he—pale, flabby, and lethargic. Sounds like an acid that dissolves blood protein or something. I've got a serious case of wan. I look like a suspended sigh. A sigh suspended by silk threads from two moths flying in opposite directions.

I must've offended Mouldie. When did he leave? He gave me the scroll and—and what? When did—he comes and he goes and only he knows the value of treasures he brings. He enters and leaves and he never sees—he sees everything. What strings he attaches to me. Dangles me from his absurdities and his belief in his own wisdoms. I guess I'm a sucker for that kind of thing. What's the difference, believing in sidewalks or Mouldie's absurdities . . . wordy absurdities. Who am I to cast a stone at nonsense? What's today if not nonsense on anyone's scale? The hell with scales, the hell with anyone, the hell with nonsense. The hell with this stupid mirror. Christ, what made me put feathers on it? That's something a crazed old lady in Duluth would do . . .

I spend half my time doing ridiculous things and the other half undoing them.

Grandmère's the furthest absurdity. Grandmère, superannuated starlet, old fool, you betrayed me. You bided your time, you waited for the perfect chance to get me, didn't you? All you demanded of me were questions all those years, and I refused to ask anything.

. . . Now, I'm not asking, I'm begging, I'll pay any price, I'll listen to your stories gladly, even the ones that I know will make no sense whatever, I'll record your every word on a tape-recorder, I'll film you, I'll book Madison Square Garden for you, Grandmère, anything, just don't be indifferent now. Jesus. Some people really change when they're dead.

Formletter. My own great-great-grandmother is betraying me.

That sham Mouldie is betraying me. This mirror is betraying me. It hangs here and absorbs every shred of happening in this room, it absorbs me when I confront it, when I laugh, it's a silent-film parody of laughter, when I cry, tears show on it but are dry when I reach out and touch it, it mentions every knot in my hair, every shadow under my eyes, it describes a look in my eyes that is NOT there, it's holding up a ghost to me, it's not even subtle, it's stagewhispering gossip that isn't true, it's, they're rumors, incredible, telling me rumors about myself, now, this very minute, just look at it betraying me.

Using the sleeve of her thin dress, she wiped and rubbed at the mirror, trying to clear the surface. But it was clouded not with soot or smoke, but with age. Time had dulled it and her sleeve was useless. Her thoughts were rising in pitch, like a voice—she was getting silently strident; bits of her thoughts began tumbling out, mumbles dropped haphazardly around her. She stared into the mirror, wiped at it, stared, wiped:

Even time, time can't be counted on for anything. It doesn't go on like a ticking metronome, that's a large lie, that whole clock business, how does it account for days that take minutes and seconds that swallow a week? How does it account for déjà vu? For time warps? For minutes that run backwards? Maybe time isn't the traitor, it's clockmakers, and those who pray to them. Well, I've stopped being fooled by clockmakers. And I've surrendered to time. I've learned to do that much . . . why wear my life out fighting it.

I'll float on it like a current, I'll swirl in its whirlpools and doze in its eddies, I'll hitch rides on its crosscurrents and see where they take me, I'll wander into its sidepools of the past without complaint or worry, I will, I'll hurl over future rapids as bravely as possible, and even when I'm in the midstream of normal Now, will I bitch? No. No. I remember when I wore a watch.

God, I—it was so amazing, just amazing. Ticked along so predictably, just slogged its little hands around its numbers. That watch had no imagination . . . it was like a mileage marker down the middle of the midstream. Who cares how many feet and miles the stream is long, who cares . . . wouldn't acknowledge all the other stuff that was happening . . . that watch's blindness really got to me. What tunnel-vision. Gross stupidity. Wonder if they'll ever come up with a watch that really keeps track of what is really happening, a sort of three- or six-dimensional watch . . . buy one in a minute. I would. Buy one in a minute. Minute. Minute. Minute. Minute. Minute, it.

Add that to my list. Watches. People believe in watches. Just like sidewalks, no difference. What enormous trust. Why can't I trust like that? I wouldn't be here if I could believe in sidewalks or watches. Or mirrors. Or therapy, be it freudian, reichian, jungian, vaticanian, or drugs, whether it's peyote, mellaril, chrystal, aspirin, or camomile tea.

Why can't I believe in turnstiles? Or fruit that suffocates in plastic packaging? Or the best-seller list? Or communes? Or christmas cards? Why can't I believe in this parody of me in this mirror? What a broad caricature it is. Definitely drawn by a self-trained hand . . . traces of an ascerbic wit there, got to credit whoever with that much, a little sloppy though, no real effort went into that image. Lazy genius, and that's profane. Better than mundane, anyway . . . profane distain, it'll stain the eyes irrevocably with fantasy production—an instant clue flashing out to bored passers-by: *Detour advised. Erratic behavior imminent.*

What a herding reaction that's always caused in me . . . herding my mind and moods into cynicism, and well, increased fantasy production too, I guess . . . each one telling the other, more annoyed each year, Move over for chrissakes you've got the whole mind-bed.

Well, the bed. The mind-bed's getting lumpy lately. Time to turn the mattress over, or junk it. Let those silver-lid tycoons dump it in the truck with the grapefruit rinds. Lumpy stained ticking bouncing off to ignominious bed-death. And take the mirror while you're at it. And the cartoon creature hovering in it, why not throw that in too. You might see the humor in it, who knows?

Mouldie knows. Where the hell is he? Never here when I need him. Betrayal's not as bad as desertion. My god, how horrible if I mean that. Have I lost my last shred of pride? How many seedy little convictions like that are lurking around like dustballs in my corners . . . window casually opened just a slight crack, and—and—dormant dustballs spring to life. How many and what are their names?

I've got to start tracking them down, this is getting ridiculous, they're suffocating me, I'm developing allergies. I don't know. You get rid of one, a new one starts forming in its place . . .

It must be the light in here. My eyes can't look quite like that. Those old dolls, hard heads and arms and soft bodies, collectors' items now, old dolls with glass eyes, look like they're bright with t.b. or some victorian thing . . . if you drop them, those dolls, one or both eyes, always, o god, they always fall back forever into the doll's head.

They never come out again. You just hear them, rattling

softly . . . muffled inside. Tiny clunks. Drop them it happens, or if you're mildly sadistic you can poke them back in with one finger. Pop. Pop clunk. Pop clunk. Smiling blind doll, funny, no, not at all funny, macabre how the smile changes as soon as you do that. Gets desperate and brittle and . . . stupid. Probably something about counterpoint being lost or something. Those holes develop their own wisdom though, o yes they do. Chilling wisdom. Accusatory wisdom. Shotgun accusatory wisdom, not just aimed at the culprit, the abuser, that's just it, that's the dreadful awful part, it's aimed like a scream at everything it can connect with.

No.
Those glass eyes. My eyes can't look quite like that. It's the glow from the coal, it does things no other form of lighting can do . . . I can wink. Or at least blink. I can blink, yes. Glass eyes can't blink. Not . . . that kind, anyway. Anyway there's no eternity of emptiness for them to fall back into, even if someone dropped me on the floor . . . anyway, who could, can, drop me on the floor . . . there isn't, there isn't an eternity of emptiness for them to, an emptiness for them to, no.

•   •

Varia was pacing now—slipping past the windows, gliding past the furniture, avoiding the mirror, carving a course through her personal aether. Chainsmoking. Even the brandy, the coffee, were forgotten now, only the smoking was left.

"I've really got to, I've got to get out of here . . ."
"Why?"
"CHRIST! I wish you wouldn't—keep popping up like that!

It gives me the creeps."

"Why?"

Seeing the stone in the glass on the sink-counter, Mouldie removed it from the water and casually dried it on Varia's quilt.

"Look—Mouldie—I've got to normalize something in my life, I mean some little part of my daily existence has to make sense, I've got nothing to hang on to, I mean Grandmère's betraying me, I simply wasn't prepared for a lousy formthing from a blood relative, and you keep spooking the hell out of me the way you—"

"Please call me M . . . I've asked you so many times, my dear. And one tirade from you per day is the quota I allowed you, so we'll have no more of this. Now. Look at us in the mirror. Come on, look, there's a girl, now don't we just look—come on, don't be petulant, where's my sweet little chickadee? Don't we just look perfect together? Sort of bobsy twins, à la Albee, wouldn'tcha say? Hmmmn?

Ah, Varia, Varia. What patience you require, you're so unevolved.

What a primitive and troubled psyche. What dissipated yet evident beauty. What whimsical yet manic hair. What a sensual yet cynical mouth. What a sexy yet bitter voice. What a—"

"Stop it. Stop it. STOP IT. I don't want to hear that shit anymore. Three MONTHS. My *god.* Three months. You said you'd help, you said, you keep saying, you know things I don't know, you'll help me get to the heart of this . . . thing . . . that's why you're here, that's—Look, if I want somebody evaluating me, or—or aligning themselves with me, I can go back to L.A. or New York, I don't need to be here with you for that. I can go to a psychiatrist for that kind of bullshit. I can go to a man for that."

"I AM a man, so don't verbally or otherwise castrate me, if you don't mind. Such abuse . . ."

"You're *not* a man, for chrissakes, you're crazier than I am if that's what you think. How can you help me know what I am

102

if you don't even know what you are? You're—a figment—
you're a—well, I don't know what you are but I don't want to
play Gretel to your Hansel at any rate. Nor a Mary
Magdalene to your Jesus. I—look Mouldie, stop it, FUCK IT
will you leave my hair *alone?* Look you said you could teach
me something, but not like a teacher; you said all these
intriguing things and all I've gotten so far is . . . promo-
tional material for god-knows-what. You're acting so suspicious, you're *making* me suspicious of you, and I've already
learned the hard way to distrust so many things . . . please, I
don't want my feelings about you to turn into common
paranoia. Anyway, I don't think I could stand one more
disappointment. Anyway, you wanted me to look at us in this
mirror? Alright, fine. *You* look. See my eyes? They didn't
used to look like this, I swear they didn't. Before you knew
me, they looked . . .
however they looked, but it wasn't like this. Look at them
now—you know those old dolls, the ones where if you drop
them, they, their eyes, they fall back—they do, that's what
they look like, my eyes—bobsy twins, ha, we look like two
inmates of the Snakepit, doll inmates, stuffed bedlamites,
wind us up and our eyes fall into eternity, yours too, look at
them . . . They're just like mine, aren't you worried? Don't
you *care* if they fall back into forever, doesn't anything matter
to you?"
"O yes, my dear, one thing matters to me. Your happiness.
My eyes can, as you so colorfully put it, fall back into
eternity; for that matter, so can my fingers, so can my private
parts, and I'd bid them adieu with absolute grace and a
mellow wave of my hypothetically-impaired hand. If it would
ensure your ease of mind, your joy, I'd sacrifice any old thing.
I'd never again do W. C. Fields, my prime amusement, if—"
"What are you doing? No—o honest to god, why are you
shrinking down? No, please don't . . . I'm calming down,
see? Don't go away right now, Mouldie, come on—"
"No my dear, I'm obviously a threat to you right now, or else
you wouldn't've questioned my manhood. One thing I know

is women. Goodbye, Varia, for a little while, I'll just hobnob about with the crumbs on the table til you pull yourself together a nit. That is, a bit. A parting word though. You are learning, my love, you are . . . that business about dolls' eyes wasn't bad, not bad at all, no need for negatives though, got to get a more positive approach to the whole thing, dolls' eyes are somewhat negative for my taste.

Brings my good spirits down, just a nit down. Bit down. You are learning, though—you just can't see the improvement since you're in the middle of yourself, but trust me, trust me . . . trust meeeeeeeeeeeeeeeeeeeeeeeeeeeeeeeee"

"Mouldie?"

•   •

eeeeeeeeeeeeeeeeeeeee

"Christ, the teapot. Waterpot. Coffeepot. Shit. Burned. How many times have I gone from the mirror to the stove, poured coffee, then to the table, pulled out a chair, sat down little jack horner style, stared out the window, got up, gone to the mirror, questioned the feathers, questioned my face, my eyes, back to the stove, back to the window, checked outside, everything's as usual, it's always the same, back to the table, light up a cigarette, and on, and on, and on.

Have I reduced my life to a mindless ritual?

Just another kind of revolving door . . . what's the difference, Mouldie's smiling nothingness, my frantic pacing around this boat, or the elaborate games of the city?

My god, how long do these storms last? I swear it hasn't stopped snowing since I got here . . . three months . . . god, three months and I haven't been with a man once . . . must be some kind of record . . . probably induces madness, celibacy causes madness, scientists confirmed today . . . even Mouldie's starting to look good to me in his better

104

moments . . . it might be worth it just for the strangeness-value. Far cry from Alex to Mouldie . . . what would you think of that, Alex? I wonder what your reaction would be. Would you think I finally reached the depths, which you would, might, refer to as my own level, or would you think I must've done it for the freak-value? After all, any woman who's been with you couldn't settle for anything less, now could she? Or would you look blank and say Varia Who? Varia Who? Varia Who. Or would you come running to save me from myself? No. Scratch that as a possibility. Maybe before but not now.

My image would be all wrong for you now anyway. People get uncomfortable around someone who has old mad doll-eyes, and you can't make people uncomfortable anymore, can you . . . ah, as Mouldie would say, the price of fame and fortune . . . it's like defying gravity, being a sex symbol in the age of the antihero. Who would've thought it. Besides you, I mean. And to think I liked you in spite of the way you looked, not because of it . . . knew you when, when. When you didn't quote dialogue in conversation, or at least credited the source. When your eyes were still naked, at least part of the time. When you didn't believe headwaiters' flattery. When you thought anything could be an art. When you liked to be alone sometimes. When you thought I was witty and interesting, not a professional liability. When you wanted to take the money and run.
When you read T. S. Eliot, not the trades. When we got Irish-drunk on your first flash of money and got thrown out of that restaurant. When we thought babies were interesting ideas. When we tried to get that photo-poster of Judas Iscariot made.
When we would spend hours trying to invent new clichés that would sound old. When we thought we could affect the world, not just exploit it or deal with it. When we pretended we were poor by choice, not knowing it was true. When after liking and even loving each other for so long, we finally Fell

In Love which ruined everything.

How weird that was, chilling and incredible really . . . when our minds were on what seemed to be the same wavelength or something, we hardly spoke at all during that time . . . when the world literally, actually, physically looked different. Textures, colors, every part . . . all the tacky sentimentality in the world made sense for that while. Wasn't even tacky . . . fairly embarrassing in retrospect, though. Jesus. Prolonged state of psychic orgasm. Rough on nerves in the long run, I'm sure. Can't last.

Didn't last. Enormous resentment afterwards, god how we crumbled apart, you really hated me for that one, didn't you? All the king's horses and all the king's men . . . Implore is the only word, you im*plored* me with your eyes, your walk, your breathing, don't let this end, how can you let me down like this, don't let this end . . . just couldn't . . . couldn't accept the fact that some sardonic fluttery spirit descended on us and left again of its own accord.

It wasn't us, Love, it had nothing to do with us, we can't claim credit or blame for that one. Some roaming madness with an echoing giggle had a hold on us, then got bored.

That's all, Alex, that's all. It just got bored and went to find new grist for its lovemill, and left its meager traces behind, like sawdust . . . on the floor, or in our mouths and hands.

• •

She stopped pacing; a sudden cut. She frowned.

How could I get mad at Mouldie for leaving?

She climbed on the bed and rolled up into a ball, hugging herself.

How could I ask him to stay when I'm in this kind of mood . . . I'd leave too if I could, split away from myself

106

and just quietly leave for awhile. I don't want to know me lately.

The times I need someone around the most are the times I'm most horrible to be around . . . Well, the ways of human nature are convoluted, contradictory, and . . . contraband. The real parts of human nature anyway, they have to be smuggled by, disguised . . . they're illegal. Forbidden. Get your veneer set up right, make it look as genuine as possible, then try to slip some of the real stuff by before anyone catches on. Like that Spartan routine . . . doing it's okay, getting caught is the crime.

If it's not pretty, change it, paint it, turn it around, do something but don't let it just sit there in full view, breathing and bleeding so blatantly. It's disturbing. Absolutes are in bad taste . . . they must've tried to teach me that . . . be pretty, not beautiful or ugly, nice, not throbbing or raw, amusing, not hysterical or scathing. Something *must* be wrong with me . . . Alex was right. I'm like that dog that wouldn't get housebroken. Never could grasp the principle, god, that dog drove me wild.

My mind's not housebroken. O Jesus. Well, it's true . . . not only does it shit anywhere it feels like, it chews the curtains, metaphysical curtains. And slippers. My mind's chewed a lot of other people's slippers. Maybe that's what Alex was trying to say, in his nice way. I was chewing his slippers and he didn't like it. Just like he didn't like my onion strategy: around and around and in and in and in all the way to the center of whatever.

Made his eyes water, he said, whatever that meant. 'Can't you let someone else do it or leave it alone for god's sake Varia, do you have to peel away the layers of *every* situation, can't you just *enjoy?*'

Maybe he was right. Enjoy. Just relax and enjoy and maybe I wouldn't be here now . . . maybe I'd still be with him. If we hadn't fallen In And Out Of Love, that is.

Well, and if he hadn't started believing his own press releases, that too . . . I knew the aborigines were right: a photograph will steal your soul, just drain it right away, suck it right up . . . leave your eyes dead and pretty. All those pictures. Ah, Alex, that primitive soul-sucking thing—if I could've only warned you, really . . . of course, if you would've believed me, that would've restricted you to the stage, and everyone knows theatre's dead. Anyway, you wouldn't have listened, you would've gotten annoyed or worse and said I was . . .

Was that, is that, your destiny, then? To have your soul drained away like water in an unused swimming pool? Did you know how painful that was for me? What agonies I went through due to the complete dearth of plugs in that time and space of my life? Do you remember how I would sometimes look in horror, silent horror, at my empty hands, and choke up? How could I tell you what I was searching, so pathetically, for? Would you have believed me?
How could I tell you I was checking every pore, every fingernail-edge, every line in my palms—especially the heart and fate lines, o god how I plundered my heart and fate lines for you—I raped my own palms in my frenzied but always altruistic search for a plug.
Anything to stop the steady outpouring of you into eight-by-ten glossies, agents' biographies, and worst of all, those demon films, those fertile and reproducing movies, those huge pagan images of you—a sudden Golden Idol who couldn't even pray to himself anymore.
Didn't you ever wonder why I examined my hands when we went to screenings of your films? Why I cried whenever I even glanced at the screen? Why I started dropping hints about two-dimensional optic expressions? I even left eyedrops, different brands, in subtle but strategic places in your apartment. I'd die before telling you this, but I bribed your last two film-editors to let me have the out-takes of you that

ended up on their floors. I'd take them home secretly and put them on the floor of my stall-shower and pour bottle after bottle of eyedrops over them, knowing how futile it was, talk about a finger in the dike, talk about emptying the ocean with a bucket.

Intellectually I knew it was hopeless, but I had to try, I loved you. What a sad little act of love it was. I really convinced myself that destroying those out-takes in my humble ritual would somehow, in some minor way, stem the flow.

I won't even go into the number of magazines and newspapers I bought on the sly and burned, whenever they carried an interview with you. You never noticed that, did you? It never occurred to you that I was mysteriously exhausted and broke whenever you hit the papers? That I was stained with newsprint for days? My lungs looked in recent Xrays like a coalminer's, from time spent burning papers illegally in a shower within city limits.

I still cough from those episodes. I still can't bear to look at photographs of anything animate. I still gag on the smell of burning paper. Still, I wouldn't trade that time for anything . . . no-one can justifiably say, ever again, that I've never done anything for anybody.

O Alex, when I first met you . . . I gave you a dime, remember? How did I know you were between takes, that's the trouble with location shooting . . . we really thought that was funny later, didn't we?

You were a perfect wino . . . what did I know . . . my heart went out to you, I hated to see anybody *that* young and sexy-looking on the skids . . . two years ago . . . two years from that day to here.

From being two dissipated-looking but loving children to, well, you're a shiny zombie and I'm on a snowbound boat in the middle of god-knows-where. Two years from idealistic posters and dimes to awards and eyedrops. More eyedrops than awards, I might add.

Two years ago, Grandmère was still shuffling around . . . I loved it when we all talked shop, the three of us. Your gaze was still so piercing and three-dimensional, mine was still clear and healthy, the noxious fumes from burning paper hadn't reddened my eyes yet, and Grandmère's—well, who knows, at that point in her career she wouldn't take her dark glasses off at all anymore, but what did it really matter? If we'd only asked her a few questions that were important. In the long run, what are floorwax commercials next to sacred axioms of my ancestors?

You don't know, you just don't know, how we blew it, Alex. She'd sit there, hunched in her side of the booth at Cantor's, just waiting, god, I could kill myself when I think about it, she was just waiting for a meaningful question or two, a delicate probe into her reticence, a nudge in her shyness and pride. You know how she always said she didn't want to inflict herself on us. She'd just sit there in ancient dignity, chewing her bagel, or chopped liver or whatever that was she liked so much, well gumming it actually, at that point the poor old darling was pretty much coming apart physically, much *you* cared.

Well, for that matter, I wasn't as solicitous as I might've been either. How could we have been so blind?

How could we pass up a chance like that? How many hundreds of bagels did we let her eat silently? She was positively *seething* with wisdom and what did we do? Shoved more chicken-liver at her, and felt each other's thighs. And slandered our respective agents. And twice unzipped each other's jeans.

I could die of shame.

Not because of the zippers, god knows Grandmère would've cheered if we'd balled each other right on top of the corned beef and the livers, she was nothing if not liberated, but because of the lost opportunities. She gave us our chance at her knowledge, and we threw it away time and again. And now the old hag's getting her Red Revenge on me. And on you too, in a subtler and more indirect way, Love: because who can say, she might've had a quick answer or two about the soul-loss you were undergoing . . . I wonder if that's ever occurred to you? She might have, must have, seen it happening, and she probably could've stopped it, reversed it even, with three sacred words.

But we didn't ask.

So now she's chortling around her happy hunting ground designing formletters. And you're reigning over L.A., enduring parking lot attendants' blackmail so that your Ferrari doesn't get mysteriously scratched and gouged.

And I'm mumbling around this surreal boat, trying to not set my coffeecup down on any of the crumbs on the table, since one of them is apparently Mouldie, and I don't need homicide added to my list of things to feel rotten about, mumbling and realizing that it's doing me no good at all to muse about the good-ol-days with Me and Alex, Alex of the flexible hands with the extraordinary joints, Alex of the gentle smile that was mean around the edges, which definitely had something to do with your success with women, and more than a few men, Alex of the fancy, actually prime, loins, loins which drove me, among others, wild when wrapped in denim even more than when unwrapped, Alex of the wind machine, which existed only in your mind but that was enough, somehow you managed to always seem to be wandering around the moors, your hair blowing just the right amount, even when you were in the shower, even sitting in Cantor's, and later, in the dark velvet restaurants where you didn't even have to sign the check, even when you were paring your toenails on the edge of the bathtub which is the one that used to really amaze me, Alex of the artichoke leaves which you ate with the methodical concentration of a raccoon, Alex of the hay fever which only made you more mysterious and you knew it, Alex of the plain-brown-wrapped literature from the Saint Jude Club, you'd kill to get to the mailbox early on those days, Alex of the private terrors that only I knew about: the irrational fear of eventual psoriasis, the constant sense of doom about old parking tickets that were already paid, the growing paranoia about leprechauns, your thing about tin, o god, all of it, I can't stand to think about it, I especially can't stand to think about when we fucked, made love, had intercourse, had carnal knowledge of each other, balled, screwed, raped, seduced, manhandled, swivved, frigged, fugged, any of those things, each of which was so unique from its fellows, will I ever again be with a man who knows the infinite and subtle distinctions between and among them all as well as you did? I can't bear to think of how we orchestrated them all like a one-hundred-piece symphony orchestra, with you conducting, your blue ribbon fluttering proudly.

I can't bear to think of how we braided them all into our nights so cleverly, never missing a strand, making sure each one was brought in time and again, what subliminal organization we had, Sunday night we'd swiv, Monday night we'd manhandle, Tuesday night we'd seduce, and so sweatily on . . . we braided in gasping splendor for two years, til we could do it blindfolded, we could do it with one arm tied behind our collective back, we could do it better than anybody, we fused together into one oily braiding machine, moaning and sighing and pausing for cigarettes and phone calls to our agents—and my publisher—we chugged and slipped and slithered along and never missed a stitch, a strand, a piccolo note, never once until we fell In and Out of Love and that did it.

•

Now why did that have to end? Why does everything have to end? Why must the birth of each moment mean the death of the last? Why does everything seem to either explode or implode? Why does irony seem to be the basic breath and end result of all living? Could that be what they mean by the Last Judgment? The Ultimate Irony? It that's true, then all satirists must be high priests and all priests must be high satirists . . .

112

My god, what if existence as we know it is really just the exhalation of breath, the fast pushout of carbon dioxide, the barking laugh of a cynic . . . Well then it's not surprising, any of it.

It's not surprising that Alex and I ended the way we did, the irony in it might've been the closest we'll ever get to God, we might've experienced the holiness of eternity when we broke up. Our moment of playing up there in the aether with the Big Kids . . . And it's not surprising that all those men—and there were a lot of them up til now—all of them bunched together, culminating in the last silence Alex dumped on me like a waterballoon, all of them, crashing through Alex's hands onto me, a perfect drench, a wet bullseye of past experiences, a splat of champagne and laughter and macrobiotic meals and bare feet and bodies and hellos and goodbyes and crocodile-and-other-tears, all of them, it's not surprising that they ended in one compact little sputz, sacred as hell, if this conclusion I'm drawing is sensible at all.

No, it's not surprising . . . but to not BE the cynic, to not be a single cell of the cynic's being, to be just one small part of a laugh of the cynic, well, I don't know.
Some theories are best left alone.
Maybe that's how they feel about me now—Alex, Mouldie, Grandmère,—I'm a theory best left alone. Pandora's box. I've never really explored self-pity fully, I'll bet I could pick its bones clean in no time. That's ridiculous. You have to be pretty healthy to wallow in self-pity . . . you have to have a self, then you apply pity in gentle dabs, or melodramatic swipes or whatever. That done, you roll it in feathers, clip it to a willowbranch and let dry. When dry, you hold it in the left hand and fluff its feathers with the right, carefully, so as not to anger it or hurt it unduly. It bites when aroused. Lewis Carroll quotes, mumbled soothingly, combined with the light fluffing procedure, render it nearly hypnotized. It will then do as you direct it to. If ethical, you will direct it to the closest

universe of floating propositions, where it will make its home.
It will flap happily—

She drew her fingers slowly across her forehead. No . . .
She slid off the bed and walked shakily to the mirror.

Well, that's fine. I can see I'm doing fine. Mirror mirror on
the wall, who's the fairest . . . who's the fair . . . mirror
mirror . . . I'm doing just fine. I can see I'm doing just fine,
well I will be doing fine, that why I'm here, that's why
I'm . . . mirror mirror . . . cracks and feathers glued to a
stranger I don't think I know . . . don't believe I've had the
pleasure . . . I don't think I know you . . . I don't think I
want—
"Listen, kid, a cuppa hot coffee's what you need. Fix you up
in no time. Why I remember in Casablanca—"
"Mouldie, you're back!"
"Call me M. . . . you never know who's listening."
"Alright. M. Bogart's not your strongest point, but I'm glad
you're back anyway. Uh, listen, Moul—uh, M, will you get
rid of the mirror for me? Just dump it over the side or
something, will you, I really don't need a mirror, actually I
don't like that mirror anymore at all, I hate it—"
She flashed him a brittle smile.
"What! A bad Bogart? You must be kidding. I do a better
Bogie than—where's your critical taste? What do—"
Varia was struggling with the mirror, trying to lift it off its
hooks on the wall.
"Mouldie, please. This damned thing's too heavy, I can't do it
alone—"
"Ach! Criticism and demands! Demands and degradation!
Menial labor, soiled hands, and hum*iliations!* In your
currently wasting body do you have one crooning lullabye,
one stroke for my fevered brow? No. I think I'll zip off to less
hostile quarters—o now stop. Stop. Sit and calm and slow
down. Stop. Ach. When I took you on, did you warn me of

this? No. I innocently believed that I would be the cubscout leader on your spiritual quest, not a wetnurse for your hysterics. Look, let's drink our coffee and be reasonable. I'll get rid of the mirror later, for right now I'll cover it with your shawl, see? Look, Varia, all covered up, can't see a thing of it, now can you? Eh? Eh? *Eh?"*

"What are you babbling about? I'm not hysterical, I don't need a nurse, wet or otherwise, I simply asked you to help me move a mirror, that's all, just . . . move a mirror, just throw a mirror overboard, is that a big deal? I mean, you claim to be a man, in fact, the whole issue of whether or not you're a man seems pretty close to your heart, you claim to be a man, and most men would help most women throw a mirror over-board, that's all. And not only am I not hysterical, I'm not even tense or crying, or if I *seem* to be crying, it's just my face that's doing it, I don't feel like I'm crying, I mean, inside I'm not crying. I'm not surprised actually if my face seems to be crying—I don't think it's mine anymore anyway. I'm serious. There's a stranger in the mirror and I don't like her, she gives me the creeps, look at her, she's hiding behind that shawl, for all I know she's laughing at me for crying.
And it's not even *me* who's crying, although she doesn't know it, it's *her* face that's crying like this.
So I get to not only have her fucking face stuck to me, but she thinks it's FUNNY. And now you've given her my shawl. Who's side are you on, Mouldie? You've betrayed me and deserted me already, and I've forgiven you out of need and largesse, mostly need I'll admit, but now if you're going to add conspiracy, double-agentry, treachery, and tongue-forking plots to the pain you've inflicted on me, well then, what can I say?"

"Your great-great-grandmother's right, Sweetums. You're not much fun at all anymore."

"Wait a minute—you know Grandmère? You talked to her? When? What did she say? Why didn't you tell me?"

115

"Well, ma petite chicorybean, in exact reverse order—I didn't tell you because it's a point of high honor with me not to involve myself in family squabbles, quarrels, or scrabbles. I include scrabbles since most gnashing is done on verbal levels within families like yours, families that value articulation above retribution or justification or ramification or anything else regarding tribulation, don'tcha know, no indeed, never in that business will you find old M, nor will you find me inserting myself like a sandbag between two female pumas aglow with bloodlust—"

"Look, all I want to know is—"

"—aglow with bloodlust as I was saying, you and your charming Grandmère of course I mean, nobody with half a mind would meddle with two ladies of high intensity and low tolerance levels, certainly not this old kid. I wouldn't touch your relationship with Grandmère with a plastic poker, no sandbag with a poker, I, that's why I didn't tell you, and anyway, second point—still going backwards, are you with me, dumpling?— what she said was you're no fun at all anymore which I already told you. Also she did say some other things in Iroquois which I, being multilingual, as I'm sure you've noticed, understood in a flash but unfortunately can't translate for you, since it would lose something in the transition, besides which it was confidential, forgive me Love, I know how that tortures you, but I'm helpless, and umm— yes I talked to her, and what else did you ask? Ah yes, why yes, I know her."

"So it's true. You and Grandmère have been mumbling around some ethereal closet together. Been exchanging trade secrets, right? Feeling smug about knowing something I don't know, huh? Tell me, Mouldie, do you have a pact with her? A pact about keeping me in the dark? Did she put you up to this? Are the two of you sitting in some bleachers watching my anguish? Why? Why Mouldie? If you would just give me one minor but important bit of information, some obscure cornerstone, I'll do the rest myself."

"My dear, every time I give you a tidbit you either don't understand it—je ne sais pas how many times my casually dropped pearls have been thrown out with the cigarette butts by you—or you don't even acknowledge that I've given you anything at all. You claim your hands are empty just when I've filled them to their ignorant brims. For instance, a *très* important secret is hovering there behind that shawl and what do you care? You ask me to heave it overboard. Cowardice. Pure cowardice on your part. You haven't the, how you say, balls, to confront and accept the reality in that cracked mirror . . . No, my dear, I'm afraid it's a real psychic faux pas to ask me to throw it overboard. A definite demerit. Your stock just went down. All of that, ah yes, all of that. My, how you can depress me. Varia, my love, at the moment you're decidedly more actress than poet. Actress without a script, which is unfortunate but not the main point. Varia the poet causes me heartache and frustration, but Varia the actress causes me to dissolve in ennui. Ho hum. Adieu."

Varia watched Mouldie dissolve into a small pool in a saucer on the table. She closed her eyes and clenched her jaws, but didn't say anything.

•   •

She sat down heavily in the chair by the table, sighed, and carefully pushed the saucer away from her. She stared at the glowing stove and lit a cigarette.

So now it's bigotry against actresses . . . that old puddle of warm jello is feeling superior to me because I've been in front of a camera. What's the difference, a poetic actress or an acting poet? . . . Anyway, the fact that I've acted doesn't make me an actress anymore than the fact that I've written obscure words makes me a poet.

What is that whatsisname—said—'Poetry is a verdict, not an occupation' . . . Verdict. Too many verdicts let loose on the world as it is . . . what I need isn't a verdict, I need some glue to hold this day together somehow, or else some dynamite to blast it apart. But to sit here suspended in this white silence . . . to smother in a snowstorm . . . will it ever stop? I'll be out of supplies soon . . . a week, ten days at best. Jesus.

Where the fuck does he get off? Stirring up trouble with the mirror and me. Got to cut down, if I keep smoking at this rate I'll be out of cigarettes and into withdrawal symptoms within days.

(Out of the corner of her eye, she saw her reflection in a tarnished silver bowl on the table.)

Do I really look like this? Or do I just think I look like this? Is my mind playing tricks on my body, or is my body playing tricks on my mind?

Even I'm not above suspicion now. What if I'm sabotaging myself . . . part of me making plans for a takeover. Well god, how strange that would be . . . what if the actress part has taken over my body and the poet part's taken over my mind. Or worse, what if the actress part's taken over my mind and the poet's got my body. Hopeless, then. Although there would be a certain charm in a poetically disintegrating body. Russian heroines. Wuthering Heights. Previously-brilliant-anything-coming-undone's always poignant.

More charm in that than in the actress-mind business . . . what if this is all a conglomeration of bits of old obscure dialogue I've forgotten? Just a part I've pieced together that's not real? What if it turns out to be a minor part? What if I write myself out of the script? What if the editor cuts me out later? What if Mouldie's right and I don't have a script at all? That would make this improvisation. Which brings it all straight back, well, not exactly straight back, sort of circuitously back to reality of some sort. And to be realistic, I haven't even worked for awhile . . . what, three months, six months . . . but how could I work when Alex and I ended? It's no wonder . . . all my time and energy just *shot* from trying to save him from some Faustian existence. Wasted. Well. Save me. Now it's time to save me. Can't save anyone else anyway. Can't save them from what they want at any rate. I want to save myself from what I *don't* want. Which I guess is—this goddamn static snowstorm and a mirror full of malevolent strangers who've hi-jacked my face. I want crickets.

I want to see what phase the moon is in, I want those snowclouds to break up so I can see with my own eyes, I don't want to have to look in a book to see where the moon is tonight. I want to be able to deal with streetlights, or else be able to not *have* to deal with them, I want to be able to face them anyway. I want to know which part of me's the poet, if any part of me is . . . or has Varia the actress worked her perfect cannibalism on that too . . .? I want Mouldie to refrigerate himself or whatever it is he has to do to solidify again, I don't want a spiritual puddle for company. Shit. (She poked at the liquid in the saucer with her finger.) I want Grandmère to send me a key, any key, that'll unlock this snowstorm, this . . .

There was a time I had keys, little keys for little rooms. Small keys for small needs. But I had them. I had my body, my senses, to unlock a room—the first one I came to, a room of simple pleasures. My mouth learned the special secrets of cotton candy and apples, my nose tracked down beef roasting, and christmas eve, nothing else has the scent of promise of chirstmas eve . . . my body wielded itself early against the wind and sun, it rolled through waves of sensations, my body grew clever at finding hands to touch it into ecstasy, my ears collected music like a beachcomber, my hands found surprises in marble, weathered wood, abalone shells, my eyes pried good news from clouds sheltering a sunset, from cities that looked vulnerable and wistful at dawn, from squirrels, from metal rusted into beauty.

Now that I think of it, that one was pretty easy to open. But then, the room of people wasn't that hard, either, and it was interesting in there . . . the overstuffed raggedy ann huggables, the tiny wind-up metal ones, the larger-than-life-size cardboard cut-outs, always smiling, the cheshire cat flashing ones, the bright highstrung mimes who showed me why they ate butterflies, the solemn mole types who proclaimed things, the frightened ones who came out only if you sang softly and didn't look, the ones who made almost imperceptible movements that everyone watched, the ones who gestured frenetically but nobody saw, the enameled ones who whirled and whistled, the unfinished ice-cream-cone ones who melted before completion, the multicolored ones who had mastered the art of constant change, the ones I can't forget and the ones I can't remember, they were all in there, and all I needed for a key was interest, humor, cleverness sometimes, with a kind of love at the core. Even when I misplaced that one, that key, I knew I'd find it again before long. I usually did. And I had hard work and luck, wrapped around acting, to get me into the room of worldly success . . . at least a little way in. Far enough to see and touch a bank balance with a lot of zeros, a name that's connected with mine and dropped by status-seekers, disposable houses and a litter of cars at my disposal, a gaggle of sycophants at every turn, charitable organizations with guilt crowbars at work, gifts and favors asked and offered increasingly, unceasingly, domestic help who steal the silver and reporters who steal privacy . . .

Alex and Grandmère walked in front of me going into that room, and I only got a step or two past the doorway, but I did see them disappear into the depths of it.

And all the weird rooms, the ones not everyone wants to see . . .

The room of excess, Christ how I loved the anarchy in that, the defiance of all laws of nature and society. That room overflowed with possibilities . .`. unusual dosages of drugs that floated me into a wordless nirvana and almost oblivion, absolute seas of alcohol that seemed to lick the world with bittersweet flames of rage and love and song, speed that exceeded everything but death wishes with cars, skis, boats, privately chartered rollercoasters, horses denounced as mad or at least wild, anything that went FAST—does it go faster than it normally should? Then let me on it, in it, give me two if it'll double the speed, slip it a pill, change the gear ratio, anything . . .

Even good books, serious reading could be perverted when I went into that room . . . nonstop wordsoaked marathons . . . offerings of great minds consumed one after the other, no pause, no time for reflection, just words swilled down for days and nights running, mixing and scrapping together in my mental stomach like a maniac's smorgasbord consumed eagerly, great volumes of wordstuff replacing eating, sleeping, fucking, I'd come out of those binges exhausted, and remembering nothing.

And sex. The celebrations, the endurance tests, the noble and not-so-noble extremes inherent in the nature of the act . . . its cyclical format: how far can you push its timing? How tightly paced, how close together can the cycles be and still work? How drawn-out and extended, like worked taffy, can they be without breaking or fading? How many people—and how few—can there be in one act of sex, rather than several copulations going on simultaneously, what are the possibilities in balloons and donuts, sexually, before the element of farce becomes an issue? How much honey can one lick off a human body without collapsing, or gaining weight?

The only key needed for that room was the willingness to run amuck.

And the strange eerie room of illness . . . where the usual proportions and proprieties in life suddenly shift. Where the world is seen through a transparent gell of a malfunctioning body—the word *mortal* assumes meaning then, and there's an opportunity to admire all sorts of intricacy . . . of the workings of the healthy world, of the body, of the different viewpoints various sicknesses offer: pneumonia sees the world through a gauze of delicate victorian blue; kidney infections look out from a flashing orange light; gonorrhea, once it's erupted in a woman like Vesuvius itself, puts the world slightly out of focus beyond a smoking, burgandy colored lens. Strange room . . . The only key needed is a badly organized line of defense, and a talent for fever.

And the room of creative wonders: another strange small room not everyone gets into. But the lucky ones who do— that room pulsates with something eternal, is lit up like a neon slot machine hitting jackpot, delivers the most expensive thrill in existence, gathers together essential and mystical beings and lets you touch them for a minute, grants your soul total relief, allows you to tapdance with past and future races, invites you to probe into hidden recesses for goodies, and suggests you make the most of it all while you're in there, because you can only stay a minute anyway. The only key for that one is an insane trust in a gift of some obscure gods, and slavish work between visits.

Well, I've searched all these small rooms and they've been fun and interesting and important enough at the time, but they aren't it, they aren't the big room with the big key, and although I know there's a big room, where the fuck is the key? Mouldie's got it or Grandmère's got it or it's on this boat . . . I'm sure it's in some haystack of important secrets, that's easy enough to figure out, but if I can't find the haystack, how can I—

There was a time I thought I had an endless supply of keys, I didn't know how few they really were—

There was a time I could find Grandmère by merely following
her trail of spilled scrubbing-water and echoed chants—as
long as I knew which building she was working at the time—
there was a later time when I could find her by calling any
gossip columnist in town—
There was a time I thought the gods knew what they were
doing.

●   ●

Between the prayers and the bleeding is something that passes
for lies or true vision or madness . . . a strung-out spun-
glass phase denied sleep or enthusiasm. Or boredom even. I'm
ticking too fast to be bored, my eyes are unnaturally wide,
strain shows. Brittle sponge absorbing.
I can feel tiny revolutions of diamond wheels polishing me—
or is that, grinding me down? All depends on the viewpoint
taken, and my perspective bobs about like a liberated
balloon; therefore I can and do take every viewpoint
available. Some curious views from strange places due to my
private winds. Float. Float and spark under the grinding
drillwheels. Nifty trick I'm capable of performing daily. I
have to credit me as I would credit a kite for its brilliant drift
on dubious winds.

Or maybe a simple psychic grenade has shattered me into
senseless complexities.
That's what Alex would say. Shattered. And Mouldie—well.
So I guess when it all comes down, it comes down to this:
sidewalks and agents and the national budget won't graft
onto Mouldie or time warps or spiritual probes or secrets. I
have tried and failed.
Failed grafter.
I just can't lay one category of reality on top the other and
carry them successfully through my life, fending off loaded
metaphysical pingpong balls with my elbows . . . I may as

well admit it—I'm totally untalented in that respect. And now I don't think I care. Because that's like a minor talent for shoplifting . . . you can survive that way for awhile, but in the long run you burn yourself out with nervous exhaustion . . . you definitely live longer if you're a hardcore beggar or a regional manager for orthopedic shoes.

So one layer or another is always slipping off me . . . but why is it always sidewalks? I have a trail of broken and decomposing sidewalks behind me . . .
And now the secrets . . . I can feel them getting farther away, not closer. The chance of finding them, of knowing them, dropping away, a dead leaf.
All the layers, by now . . . all of them fallen and strewn behind me.

•   •   •

"My dear, you look desperate. Unfortunately it's singularly unbecoming to women, desperation. Penultimately unattractive, as it were."
Mouldie was suddenly sitting on the bed, an ivory cane balanced on his knee.
Varia stared. "Are you trying to . . . *jolly* me out of this place I'm in, or are you really—that—"
"I'm trying yet again to get you to grapple with reality, for your own present and future welfare. Now look, Fuzzywraithe, I've just learned that there are some other places I must go to immediately, some other things I must attend to—
"No! Mouldie for god's sake—if you leave now, what'll I—I mean, maybe now that you're back—if you go, what'll I—"
"You will most likely cancel your melodramatic self-indulgence, shuffle off in your rowboat, find a sensible apartment in New York, and become a cashier in a chain supermarket."
"I guess you really *are* an asshole. You're just like this fucking

snow. You make everything—"
Varia turned to the window across from the bed, to illustrate
her point.
"—look! Who the—it's a *kid*—look Mouldie, there's someone peeking in, it's a face—LOOK for chrissakes, will you—"
(Mouldie was studying his cane) "there's someone—"
"Babydoll, Chickaroonie," Mouldie slid off the bed and
turned Varia gently but firmly, holding her arms, while
stroking her face, her hair, with one almost-free hand. "—
Babyduck, I can't stay long, I told you that, but I can't leave
you in the grips of a—delerium trembly, a . . . well,
Sugarnose, a hallucination. You've been at your brandy,
haven't you? Or was it a pinch of opium? Hmmn?"
Varia struggled to turn.
"But how'd a kid get—"
Mouldie held fast. "Now stop it, Varia, you're embar-
rassing me beyond—"
Varia, starting to cry in frustration, insisted, "God, LOOK,
Mouldie! See it?! Look at his eyes! And his mouth—his
smile—that's—please, look, his mouth alone—it can save me,
I know it, he's—glowing!"
He wouldn't let her turn her head back to the window. His
hands were clamps, his eyes steady. But he crooned softly at
her:
"No, Varia, your madness won't save you. You can imagine
whatever you please . . . it's a child? Alright, Raggy Lady,
there's a child out there . . . but he's really up here, angel—"
(He poked her temple with a forefinger) "—and you can
hallucinate whatever your exotic little imagination pleases,
but try this: imagine a decent man, a solid hubby, a diapered
child that's *real,* that's peanut-buttery and yours, and a job, a
condominium with a respectable mortgage; dream up off-the-
rack clothes, t.v. dinners, calling your mom to chat, gaining
twenty pounds of flesh and thirty pounds of Team Effort—
use your vivid powers of conception *constructively.* Use it to
decipher the wisdoms I've showered on you—"
"No. This can't be my imag—*it can't.* O my god—"

He pulled her to his chest and clamped her there with his arms.

Varia closed her eyes tight and began muttering, as though praying:

"She races, a nameless egghunter, on spindle legs, on diphthongs and far dawns—"

Mouldie was listening intently, but not to her. He said, "But I agree! Our frail and frenzied lady is indeed tedious. She carps. She snaps at the very hand that doles out solace. You must all be outraged at the way she treats me. She's a little slow on the draw, psychospiritually speaking—"

"—gleam-eyed wakeling, she races clutching an empty jug—"

"She rages and sulks around her pathetic little boat like a common manic-depressive, lamenting her past, despising her present, denying her future—"

"—silver, clay, opals, feathers, veins, tears, brass, blood, fearcries form it, form the shell—"

"—all this, it breaks my heart, but all this is true. However, Seedy Varia does have certain things that weigh in her favor . . . to wit—"

"—who could bear it? The weight, what emptiness fills it—"

"—one, she is, in a sense, the new girl in town. Well, if not in town, then on this bay where I happened to find her. Two, she is a willing morsel for my famous curiosity. Three, she's very earnest, yes she really tries—"

"—watch: her legs aquiver, racing, racing, a hollow begs eggs—"

"—four, she sometimes makes good coffee, five, compared to the two strangoes I met this morning—"

"—a vacuum sucks warnings at her: run, egghunter—"

"—this chick is Queen of the Hop."

"—run egghunter, I NEED!"

•

"What you need is to get yourself fu— You need a man,

126

darling, a man. Why don't I know that a woman, when most unappealing and fretful, why that's when she needs a man the very most. I'll even postpone my important engagements for a wee while for you, since—lucky for you—I just happen to be right here and reluctantly willing. My card is blank for the next dance, as it were. 'Course I am a bitty tad pooped, having driven wild two ladies in the last twenty-four hours . . . Your sainted great-great-grandmama I mean, and a sexy little dancing girl I met on the beach this morn. G-string was all the little minx—"

"I need. I need. I need . . ."

Varia's eyes opened and shut like a camera lens, in synch with her words. "I am egghunter, crippled by a knowledge: people's lives die of fright daily. I can't unknow it, so little I know, how black to know that, o I need to unknow it—"

"—mature girl she was, but what a body. Had a lovely brunch, then left her writhing in ecstasy, I did. On pebbles I believe. Squirming on pleasure-pebbles. Poor dear. But— there's enough to go around, Lovey, just lift your torn hem." Varia gazed at him, unblinking, hands limp. She mumbled:

"—die of fright. Afraid the face in the window is really not." Mouldie propelled and shovelled her towards the bed, explaining:". . . bad back you know . . ."

Varia lay there, quiet as defeat. Mouldie stepped to the sink, poured olive oil into his ungloved hand, spun back to the bed, raised Varia's dress, and spread oil on her thighs, groin, belly, as though he were applying wallpaper glue to paper.

"Since I can postpone my plans, as I told you, but not cancel them, I only have time to prime your primary erogenous zones, my dear. No time for frou-frou's today. Tiddleywinks with the titties. None of that. Just a bang. But then that's what you need, eh?"

He sputtered his fingers around her thighs, her navel, her numb groin, and watched for reactions.

"Don't try to be cool, Varia . . . your response is that of a crêpe-hanger . . ."
Now he brought the other hand into it, and squiggled ten fingers—gloved and ungloved—around. Varia stared at him.

"My dear, you'd never know your grandmother was a hot-blooded Iroquois. Try to remember: a million women have thrilled to these semigloved hands. A thousand turbaned chanters facing East have received Mouldie-seed gleefully. A hundred small plastic saints in '65 Chevies smile when they think of me. Uncounted magnates of Industry dream of me while gazing at production lines. Riveters claim me. Carwashes baptize my faithful. Governments honor me with Stamp and Loophole. Children debate me on eternal August afternoons. Politicians require me. Hoboes laugh at me, but who cares? Old parents quote me aloud and blame me silently. Someone hates me. Many need me. More want me. All have felt me. All have seen me. Some think they have been me, but you know, you know, they're the shrewdest and saddest and they'll never unravel it. Many know me and sigh. More try. Some I lie with. Some I don't. Greed is a password at first and an ultimate stumble at last. I travel fast like love, like the plague. I can be charmed but never fooled by my little generals. I can be stolen or broken but never earned. I can be learned but not understood. I can—"

"Then fuck me." Varia's eyes were closed, her voice flat and distant.
"Well, I see you're coming around, my drear! Having noticed my hands, I guess. Hands that've been close to more than a few crowned heads of Europe, a few sweaty heads in taco stands, why even heads of lettuce have once or twice quivered at my touch—"
"—fuck me."
"Here, try this, bit of a flourish I devised recently."
"—fuck me."
"How 'bout the Tophat Teaser, guaranteed to make you

128

crazy . . . never knew the what-for of that small brim-feather before, eh? Heh heh heh. Your grandmama's favorite, this one . . ."

"—*fuck me.*"

"If we had but a bit more time, I'd drive you straight into catatonia with this—"

Varia sat up, straight and rigid.

"—*FUCK ME.*"

"Uh, why of course, my dear, planning to, soon as I announce our change of plans and my further delay to—" Mouldie touched the top of his head, felt around, searching: he looked at his hand, warm, damp, empty.

"WHAT? What have you done, Jezebel? He's—why, he's suffered a nervous collapse. That's what you've done to him! Dissolved in hysteria, the delicate darling! What? Have carnal knowledge of the hussy who brought my protégé to ruin? Not on your life—"

"—my life's dying of fright . . ."

"O no! you'll get my pity and solace and guidance, but not my seed. You will never comprehend my grief. Nervous collapse. Oh."

In monotone, Varia said:

"People's lives die of fright. I'm running in death, sinking. Destroying your favorite something that was nothing and is nothing still. A damp forehead condemns me. Of course, I am guilty of causing a sweaty brow. Maybe. But you're guilty of emotional vandalism. . . . I don't know which is worse . . . but there's a curse on this moment. I feel it settling like heavy gases on us. Both of us. It's in our pores. We breathe clouds of it when we speak. I circulate it as I say these very words . . ." Her smile was hopeless. Mouldie was listening, his mouth pursed, watching. Varia continued:

"I've dreamed hard on perfumed aether, but I inhale a curse. And I know why now. And I know why you can't fuck me. Why you can't anything. Well, neither can I, now. But I know why."

Her giggle had no trace of humor. Her eyes glittered. She slid off the bed. Mouldie's eyes, inscrutable, followed her. She glided to the mirror, pulled the shawl down, and pointed at her reflection.

"See?" She giggled again and stepped closer to the mirror and whispered,

"Mouldie . . . . *fear rules.*"

She looked long and deep into the mirror and saw only the dark glow of a void. So she was the nightmare that fear dreamed, and that sort of dream has no reflection. She wasn't the dreamer after all; she was absolved. The void wasn't marred by the smallest illusion, it was pure, and her only obligation had been, all along, to acknowledge it, to pay it homage with her acceptance. She knew that if she still considered herself a human being, she would be in good company: others had seen and been consumed by this truth, and had passed the word. It had passed over her head, until now, but she had finally stumbled on it, alone, all by herself, and she knew that if she still considered herself human, she would be smug about that. Smug nightmare. It was better to not have to judge that image, no more appraisals, no more anything. It was better this way, she was free in her total captivity, reassured in the cliché of it: that was what made it perfect, made it bearable. She heard her master in the mirror. He trusted her, now that she understood. She loved him for his patience, his endurance of her struggles against him. She was proud, complete, dependable, because of that trust. She listened to his curse, his warning, in each breath she took, and heard his blessing when she exhaled. The emptiness in the mirror deepened and approved, she could feel it. She had obeyed so often, never acknowledging his right to rule, that had been her mistake. She'd given him so much of her life, but that hadn't been enough, now she could understand even that. He required more.

Moving jerkily, suddenly a wind-up doll, she struck the mirror with her fist. She watched it in slow motion, seeing

every path of every jagged piece as it showered to the floor. She picked up a long thin triangle and humbly, matter-of-factly, as though she were performing a familiar ritual, drew it across her right wrist, then set it back down on the floor. One edge of the shard was red. Blood streamed down her hand. She put her left hand on the bed to steady herself, and said:
"Now I know better . . . you had, have, no secrets and wisdoms to give me . . . only one. Just one terrible little law . . . and you obey it well, don't you, Mouldie? It's really just a small zany horror . . . wouldn't you say? Isn't it? Hm? I wanted to shine, really shine through some kind . . . some sort of freedom . . . and now . . . O Jesus I was so blind . . . now I know, that shine, *my* shine . . . sometimes I was afraid it was an illusion, but it's better and worse than that, o it's all too real—and something's slave—fear's slave—and you just watched me jangle my shackles . . . I didn't know what they were . . . I thought—"

She leaned heavier on the bed, tipped her head back, and licked her lips, as Mouldie watched, unmoving.
". . . *thought* . . . there's no such thing . . . when the very atmosphere has been just a curse . . . but . . . if I could've, if I could've—"
She closed her eyes, then reopened them. The dark stain on the quilt was spreading; the pool on the floor growing quickly. "—but I know better now, don't I? I know what you know . . ."
Becoming too heavy for her legs, she eased down to the floor, onto the broken glass. Mouldie was in her line of vision and she stared at him through a mist. He was still watching her, expressionless.
". . . so I'm floating, that's all, just drifting . . . now. Just a chained cloud crossing some night sky . . . your night sky maybe . . . bruised motion . . . singing low of illusions and . . . and of unfathomed depths of . . . tears . . ."
Her eyes closed, and she said:

". . . all I ever found before was an implacable confusion and . . . the useless motion of love . . . and pieces. There are still pieces in here now . . . fragments of spirit and flesh . . . dropping into this simple truth, this mystery . . . and I'm sliding through it, touching its folds and shadows . . . finally incoherent with understanding . . . in awe . . . of the knowledge that I'm near the center of a fingerprint . . . so this is where dream and reality meet . . . this is where fear rules."

•   •   •

The child with the electric hair and eyes turned away from the window. He opened his lips slightly, then closed them again, and swallowed. He jumped lightly from the edge of the rowboat—arms out, balancing—to the bottom of it. Near his foot was a gullfeather, wedged between two warped boards. He dislodged it carefully. Then scavenging around under the wooden seat in the bow of the boat, he found a candle and a few dry matches. He remembered that the old woman had mentioned earlier how well-equipped the skiff was . . . and now, squatting and bending under the seat to protect the entire operation from the falling snow, the child lit the candle, anchored it in melting wax, and set fire to the feather. It burned in small spurts, curling quickly into black lumps on both sides of the charred spine. Then leaning over the edge of the boat, he set the burnt feather on the water to float away. And he said:

"As the dharma of a feather is to fly and float, as the dharma of a god is to dispense magic, as the dharma of a demon is to terrify, the dharma of Varia was to shine through. Varia, who broke the law of her own being. Sad web-spinner, shine dimmer—"

"YOU did it! You horrid little shred of nonexistence, you frightened that poor woman out of her wits and 'round the bend—"

Mouldie had been struggling with the stuck window for a full minute, and had finally yanked it open and thrust his head out.

"—YOU! With your cute but hypocritically dimpled ass, your peeping tom habits, your weird friends—look what ya done to my baby! She's leaked all her lifedrops! She's in a puddle! You spooked her, you freakish featherburner, spooked her right off her trail."

Mouldie's knuckles were white and lumpy, gripping the sill. "And to top it all, small Fatto, my tophat fell in her puddle. You'll get the cleaning bill, I promise you!"

Mouldie then slammed the window shut, cracking the glass. The child silently considered the candle which was still flickering under the bow-seat, then picked up the oars, and standing in the middle of the boat, began to row around the stern of the houseboat.

•   •

Mouldie hooked the window shut and, breathing hard, strode to the table. He filled a china cup with brandy, turning the cup so that the chip was away from him. Sipping brandy, he turned and surveyed Varia's body, the pool she was in, the stained quilt. He shook his head sadly.

"Why must renters always make a mess? Always end up ruining a place?"

He set the cup down, after a long swallow, and bent over Varia's form. Clumsily picking her up, he staggered over to the rocking chair, in the corner by the sink. He set her in the chair, arranging her like a ragdoll, smoothing her hair, closing her eyelids. He stood back, then, squinting critically at the arrangement.

He frowned, displeased with the whole thing: the chair was too austere, Varia's body was too—disheveled. He redid it. Still not right. The third time he was satisfied. Varia's hands were folded demurely, her ankles crossed, her head nodding. She could've been napping. He went back to where she'd been lying and, stepping over the mirror fragments and pool of blood, and using only two fingers, he picked her shawl up and shook it to get any bits of glass off . . . then went back to the rocking chair and draped the shawl around her; the larger stains were hidden now. Standing back, he nodded and smiled.

Then with his foot, he touched the tip of one rocker, and set the chair in motion. It creaked and rocked slowly, back and forth. He retrieved his hat from the damp floor and, holding it away from his coat, dropped it into a dishpan of water in the sink, mumbling, ". . . probably never be the same . . ." He pressed down with his toe on the tip of the rocker again, to keep the chair going. Varia's hair and the fringe on her shawl swayed.

Mouldie went over to the table again and took another swallow of brandy . . . he held it in his mouth for a few seconds before swallowing it . . . then he set the cup down and started hunting under the bed, inside the barrel, under piles of clothes, for a broom and mop and rags. Passing by the sink, he poked at his hat in the darkening dishwater, and muttered: ". . . brimfeather's shot to *hell* . . ." He tapped the rocker again on the way by, giving it a new surge of momentum. The hair and the fringe swung faster. The creaking picked up its pace.

He peered out the window near the stove, through a hole in the lace curtain, and saw the child row past for the second time. Putting his hands on his hips, he muttered, "Why, I'll be damned. That pudgy little pile of perversity is actually surrounding me like an Indian raid . . . what a day. What a day." He finally found a broom stuck in the barrel among hundreds of yellowing issues of Variety and three or four pounds of feathers.

He began to sweep up the broken glass.

". . . take me hours to get this place ready for the next tenant . . . hours . . ."

•   •

After rowing around the houseboat three times, the child paused and became part of the quiet. He held the oars still in the water, and listened: nothing but the creak of a rocking chair, and even that was muffled by the falling snow and the distance between the skiff and the houseboat.

The creaking sound speeded up, then slowed down again. He saw a dark shape pass by one window, then a second. The houseboat bobbed in the water, gently. The tin chimney threaded smoke into the air. The chair creaked. The child breathed evenly. The candle on the floorboards of the skiff guttered, then flared even brighter. Snow fell. It was time to go.

The child looked—away from the beach he had come from, away from the houseboat—towards the other shore. He couldn't see it through the snow, but he sensed the right direction to row in. He could feel the solidity of land towards the southwest, and that's where he now pointed the skiff's bow.

As he sliced the oars through the water, he watched the houseboat grow smaller . . . and he began to speak:

"I almost heard a laugh of relief, a song beyond belief and triumph. I almost heard you, Varia, hum with understanding. I almost heard you roll my name around your mouth like bubblegum. I could've heard if you would've done.

For I hear exactly every plane of sound: I hear the heavy roll

135

and can unload the dice in every game in town. I listen with ears and eyes and more and I hear the death of coinclocks and paperdolls that flatten themselves against waking. I hear my possible evaporation in The Faithful's flaring needs. I hear the sizzle of a cynic's touch. I hear a symphony The Company's wheel reduces to a hiss. I hear the master of the wheel's turn, the eater of silent distances and lotuses, as he marches through alleys, checking.

And I hear all this under sand and over rooftops and off the wall and beside the point and on the dot and within a broken harp-string.

I hear poets whisper behind peeling doors, locked.
I hear children laugh beyond their parents' lies.
I hear seagulls complain in spite of the ocean's patience.
I hear the pulse surge inside private visions.
I hear the pulse weaken and slow within compromise. I hear the weariness of eyes as they close to minor truths. I see eyes and ears that fight each other over scraps of that truth. I see orphaned totems cut lôose in space. I see neglected kings become cruel. I see pampered beggars become crueler. I see small greeds eroding scouts. I see tumbleweeds tripping jugglers. I see magicians condemning themselves as fakes. I see frauds calling magic their chauffeur. I saw an honest man once. I see beachcombers sharing their findings. I see dogs sheltering cats from wind. I see wind cooperating with flags. I see aging bartenders trying to care. I see drunks praying accurately. I see winos watering their holiness. I see men of ambition polishing their pride on strangers' expressions. I see wavy rainbows of hot fluid motion. I taste the honey of being fluid motion. I taste the bitterness of those who didn't try. I taste the acrid ashes of those who teach vapidity. I taste the grey lumps of those who learn vapidity. I taste the sweet promises of treacle. I taste cream and know comfort. I taste war and face damages. I taste treachery and understand the abuse of salt. I taste love and savor it slowly. I taste loyalty and chew very carefully. I taste cowardice and spit quickly. I taste institutions and choke. I taste pork and drool. I taste

failure and remember the taste of tears. I taste my hand and feel cozy. I touch my tongue and dream delicatessens. I touch the stone of cathedrals and understand snowflakes. I touch delicatessen counters and understand cathedrals. I touch men and feel lightening. I touch women and feel air and earth. I touch men and grow gardens. I touch women and hear thunder. I touch credit cards and feel foolish. I touch stones and grow serious. I touch velvet and consider solitude. I touch drums and know the masses. I touch a chalice and start a party. I touch celery and feel holy. I know celery's secrets, and even now, live in its heart. I have known the simple mysteries of rock . . . rock so jagged and hard that even wine and tears glanced off. I have known sleepwalkers, stalking hopes that crept moonside. I have known Druids and their strange results. I have known

I know

I am Druid's egg, splendid in lack of symmetry, amazed at my grinning red yolk, tumbling up the glass hill, hatching and re-forming incessantly on my blue travels, my wobbling roll, my rollicking lopsidedness a constant proof of life over reason. Stasis despises me. Magic exhalts me. Cats and shamans worship me. Tax collectors fear me. Helping hands, stiff with concern, plot. For I am Shamash! And I have always released me into the custody of my own shine. I am safe from Owl tipping after me, swaying with his hazy breath, rasping theories of doom at my back. In my glow, o how I speed: a round flash. I cause him blinks and shadows he's never before seen: owlshadows, blacking grasses in the glare. In my light-dance I spin him into a lumpen softling of feathers and winking wisdom—grey talons dropped in midnight—bellfeet jigging. For I am the kid called Shamash. And I am the child called Mantra. I am the child probed for gold. I am the child poised on a coin. I'm seen by sly eyes rehearsed in aversion while I'm felt by hands that search my smile. But my smile disappoints in its perfection: for where are the breathing shadows the nameless ones need to fold into? They are there . . . there behind me, and in them are riddles and pains, webs, too: many webs with infinite spiders leering, winking. But I am Shamash, I am Mantra, I am Ernie, with a million dancing light-echoes. Above them all, my toes fly over mountains and sense and skin. Patterns dissolve beneath my spin. Behind my eyes of spangle and salt—salt of a dozen colors—I am just Ernie with a million Shamash lights and a million Mantra shadows. In them you must prance to the end of pain! In them you must sing anthems that never end and never repeat! In them you must find me with eyes and toes and groins! For with my lights and echoes, I float through sticky tunnels leaving anthems hung like moss! With them I feed the webs with breath as I shine through, I, Ernie!

part three, an epilogue/ **Even Morpheus**

Me! Ernie! Who'd you think ordered it?"
A thick arm gestured in exasperation. A hawaiian shirt flashed back the Baja sun.

The waiter came over and set the tray down on the low table in the sand.

"Use your head, fella. If you get an order for one mint julep, and you come out here and see one guy—and *only* one guy— on the entire beach, well then it figures that he's the patron who requested a drink. Jesus."

He snapped his magazine up into position and shook his head.

"Sheesh."

"I'm very sorry, sir. It's hotel policy. If one doesn't take the order oneself, one must double-check which guest ordered it when one is delivering it, so that there are no mistakes. Margueritas ending up where mint juleps belong and so forth. This hotel prides itself on excellent service. Will there be anything else now, sir?"

Ernie looked up at the waiter: balding, black suited, sincere as hell, or at least well-trained to give that impression, past retirement age by at least twenty years.

"How old are you, uh—"

"M, sir. I'm called M."

"Okay, M, how old are you anyway?"

"Why, sir, old enough to have mastered the nuances of my profession and young enough to fulfill the most strenuous of my duties, sir."

"How old, M?"

"The management prefers its employees not to give out any personal information, sir. I'm very sorry." An apologetic hint of a bow. "Will there be anything else, sir?"

Ernie went back to his magazine.

"Yeah. A less shabby backrest."

"Right away, sir."

Ernie craned his neck to watch the waiter walk heavily through the sand, back to the building. He smiled to himself, knowing M would be back in less than a minute with a backrest replacement. Not too interesting to have predictable help, but convenient. Still straining his neck, he appraised the building. Spanish and silent, everything so understated, it fairly screamed First Class. He thought he heard footsteps on a tile floor, faintly. He wondered why footsteps in expensive halls had a grand resonance, while footsteps in tenement halls were muffled little cries; even if the same feet made the same steps, even if both floors happened to be tile. One of life's little mysteries. His neck was getting sore. He uncraned it and sipped his mint julep.

He heard a trudging in the sand. Less than a minute.
"Will this do, sir?"
"Fine. Much better."
Ernie lumbered up and stood on a towel to avoid the hot sand. M replaced the first backrest with the second one, which was identical to it. Both were brand-new. Ernie lowered himself back down, heavily.
"Listen, M . . ."
"Sir?"
"Uh . . . I was hoping it wouldn't be too crowded here and all, but—I mean, is it always *this* empty?"
"Empty, sir?" M seemed concerned, but vague.
"Yes, dammit, empty. I haven't seen another guest since I got here this morning."
"Sir, it's company policy to consider humanity as being similar to the tides. Regarding ebb and flow, that is. In fact sir, the management feels—" (Here M leaned forward and lowered his voice further) "—that there's alot to be learned from the genius of tide."
He winked at Ernie.
Ernie wet his thumb with his tongue and turned the page of his magazine.
"I take it your management would consider the guest population that's frolicking on the beach today, to be at a low ebb."
M smiled politely.
Ernie said, "Okay, M, that's all. Got everything I need. Better run along before your tuxedo bleaches out. And here."
Ernie tossed a wadded-up dollar bill to M.
M caught it, tipped his head and began to plow his way through the sand back to the hotel.
Ernie ran a hand through his curly grey hair, and wondered if the mice in L.A. were playing, knowing the cat was in Baja.

143

•

Sunset on the Pacific was offered as one of the hotel's main attractions, and Ernie believed in getting his money's worth, so when he figured that the sun would be (as he put it) alive and kicking for less than another hour, he picked up the walkie-talkie that had been given to him with the beachchair/backrest that morning, pushed the button, and said, "Send some dinner down here in about an hour, would you? I'd like veal—scallopini, parmesan, roast, I don't care what style, just make it veal . . . and uh, a good rose. Oh—and bring down some candles, it'll be dark by then . . ."

A static filled pause, then M's voice:

"It would ease confusion and aid us in our attempt to give all our patrons the exquisite Old World Service we are renowned for, if, whenever you use your convenient walkie-talkie, you would state first your beachchair's number, your walkie-talkie's name, and, finally, your own name. Having given us that information, you should then immedieately go on to request the service you require at that time. Please bear in mind this is for your increased pleasure during your stay with us. Thank you."

Ernie closed his eyes for a few seconds, thought of a few statistics about middleaged men and stress, then checked the number on the beachchair's canvas back. He punched ON. "Guess."

"Sir, it's against com—"

"Awright, fucker! It's Number One, got that? And this ugly little black thing I'm holding has two things written on it: *El Hotel Quién Sabe Grandé* and *Scooter*. I don't believe it, but it says here, *Scooter*. And my name, as you fucking well know, is Little Ernie SHAMASH!"

"And how many members in your dinner party, sir?"

Ernie's finger was shaking as he held down the ON button.

144

He hunched close to the walkie-talkie, his mouth almost touching it, and hissed: *"One."*

"Now let's see. What could a Littlernieshamash be? It sounds like it might be a disposable cigarette lighter but it looks more like an enraged dumpling."
She came around from behind him and stood directly in front of him, her weight on one leg, like a Vogue model gone gunslinger.
Ernie stared and developed a slow smile.
"Well hello there. If that was supposed to be a joke, things are picking up around here. If it wasn't, they've gone from bad to worse."
"I just thought I'd flatter you, so I'd make a good first impression, that's all."
She was pale, gaunt, fragile-looking. Her hair looked like a domestic pet that had been in the wild for ten years . . . signs of its origins still barely visible, but unreclaimable. Her dress was an obviously expensive shred of gauze that had been treated like denim, and showed it. She was barefoot. Her eyes, which were almost too large, had the look of raw honesty found only in liars and lunatics, Ernie noted. He decided on liar.
"And what's your name, honey?"
After a minute, she answered him, her voice low, with rough edges.
"Very."
After a minute, he answered her.
"Well, it's cute out today. All day. Been about this cute the whole day. But I'll bite, why not? Very what?"
"Just Very. But then, we're only playing, aren't we? Or are you one of the three people in America who've never seen one of my films?"
Ernie pointed at her, and nodded.
"*Right.* I thought you looked familiar . . . you're the one in all those sort of weird movies—"

145

"Weird?" she looked at the nail of her index finger.

"Well, artsy, then. Never seen one myself, but I see the posters, you know, the ads, around all the time. Very big in L.A. Thought I'd seen you somewhere."

"And you have. Everywhere. Unless you're blind too, and then your seeing eye dog would be the one I'd be having this conversation with."

Ernie patted the sand next to him. "Why don't you sit down here? It makes me uncomfortable, you standing there like that."

"Or else you could stand up, too. Why don't you? Or is there a reason? Aha, I know. You're as short standing up as you are sitting down."

"Alright. Look, Missy. I'm attracted to girls with spunk—or as the English say, cheek—but I don't take no shit from no one. So watch your mouth or run along. It's your choice."

There was a pause, and then Very laughed, a long strange laugh. Then grabbing the walkie-talkie by Ernie's chair, she pushed the button and said: "Bring my chair, please."

M's voice crackled over the instrument:

"It would ease confusion and aid us in our attem—"

Ernie screamed toward the walkie-talkie:*"Goddammit,* ONE, SCOOTER, SHAMASH, *now bring her fucking chair!"*

"Ah, Mr. Shamash. Very good, sir." M clicked off.

Ernie muttered, in Very's general direction, "Pardon my language, but . . ."

She was staring at him in disbelief and starting to laugh again.

Almost instantly, M came lurching out of the building, the doors swinging shut behind him. He stumbled across the sand, readjusting his grip on the chair every few steps, stopping twice to catch his breath. On he came, as Very stared at Ernie and Ernie stared at the setting sun.

"Where would you like it, Miss Very?" M was panting.

She pointed to a spot next to where she stood, the spot directly in Ernie's line of vision. M planted the chair in the sand.

Ernie said, "A rocking chair. On the beach."

It was wood, dark, heavily carved, gothic. There was a flat, plaquelike area on the headrest that wasn't carved into—and stenciled on it in white paint was the name VERY.

Very floated down into the chair and arranged her gauze, saying,

"Terrific. Thank you, waiter. And one more thing—send something down from the kitchen in a while, would you? Anything at all, whatever looks good. Surprise me."

M nodded and stood waiting, his breath quieter now. The low orange sun was eclipsed for Ernie by Very and her rocker, the sun's last glow diffused around the chair-edges and streaking out into the Mexican sky. the silhouette began to move slowly, its shadow creeping up Ernie's body and then slipping back down, as Very rocked.

M's standing had turned from waiting into a state of static existence. He seemed to be growing roots, or meditating.

"Oh, sorry." Ernie noticed. "Here you go, M." He tossed another balled-up dollar bill to M, who caught it, then almost at his pocket, fumbled it. It dropped at his feet, sand immediately hiding it. M stooped and began dredging the sand with his fingers, and on the fourth pass, found the ball. After brushing the sand off, he carefully tucked it into his inner breast pocket.

Very smiled at him: "Gotta keep your rights in your constant pocket, Babe."

"Yes indeed, Miss." M turned and shuffled away then, not asking if there'd be anything else.

Very, seeing the question on Ernie's face, said: "That's the punchline of an old shaggy-dog story."

Ernie asked, "What was the story?" while he drew out of his pocket another dollar bill, new and crisp, and crumpled it up

into a ball, just in case he needed another tip for M soon.
"I don't remember, but the punchline comes in handy every
now and then . . ."
Ernie slipped the small paper ball back into his pocket.
"You're just a whole string of surprises, aren't you?"
Very rocked and regarded him. She asked, "You like
surprises?"
He shrugged. "Depends."
"Hmm. Well, I do . . . but there seem to be fewer and fewer
around all the time. Another endangered species, I suppose
. . . it doesn't really matter anyway, since how many
surprises are really surprising, right? Besides, as the old sage
said, Life Is A Process, Not A Thing."
"What's that got—" Then Ernie changed his mind and tactics.
"What old sage said *that?*"
Very's voice went flat with disdain: "Harpo Marx, of course."

•   •

Ernie sat and watched Very block the sunset. Very rocked
and watched Ernie grow orange in the sun's last intense
struggle, then dim out into shades of subtlety, as color
drained away into darkness.
They were silent as they watched the changing of time take
place.

The lack of light was suddenly so total, so dense, that it didn't
seem possible that electricity or candles could affect it at all.
Black simply prevailed. Very watched the eastern horizon, the
mountains, black on black, and said:
"It's coming. I can sniff it out." She illustrated her point by
sniffing at the air, then laughed, sounding far away. Then, her
voice developing that edge that signals a quote, she announced:
"The moon, this time, will burst."

148

As if on cue, the moon, full, popped above the horizon and its white light began fingering its way over the land and ocean. Ernie's hair became a silver explosion, his shirt a day-glo reminder. Very became a series of narrow and curved white planes, her dress a cobweb, her eyes larger than before. Her chair was a thousand highlights and shadows, a carved mystery.

"Burst?" Ernie spit the word out with a short laugh.

"That's right. If not this time, then next time for sure." Very sounded solemn and strict. "It's from one of my movies that you didn't see. It was a night scene, full moon just like this one, and we shot it on this huge pile of boulders . . . that's all there were—boulders. No bushes, nothing. Very bleak and dramatic. The wind was howling, the sea down below was crashing around, it was cold as hell, o it was so fucking cold up there. Well the point is, the guy who played opposite me had just died—you know, in the script—and I said this—soliloquy—to him. Well, it just tore everybody up, everybody who saw the film I mean . . . let's see if I can remember the whole thing . . . um. It's not really long . . ."

Ernie sat and wondered if his empire had survived his absence for a whole day.

Very paused, collecting herself, then said—

" 'The moon this time will burst . . . it has to, how can it survive its own fullness? I have to keep watch: I've been chosen by me since I'm the only one blinking and smoking in the world tonight.

Everyone else is sleeping or on some further beach dancing in the sand . . . two people somewhere—I swear I saw them, Love, were welding and flowing into each other's glimmer; they did it for us; dancing by proxie; they kept exact time with the silence, not missing a shimmer. I meant to call out a Bravo! but couldn't of course. My responsibility was to the moon, and I'm no shirker. . . . So I watched perfectly as the moon grew more turgid. And I listened perfectly as your

sleep deepened into a death. I was very busy.' . . . And then
the camera pulled back slowly, and I was just sitting there
staring up at the moon, smoking a cigarette, and gently
patting the leading man's head . . . well, that's it."
She waited.

"Yeah. That's very—nice. Say, do you happen to know what
time it is?"
"No, did you catch the tense change? That's what gives it that
sort of surreal quality, that strange impact—"
"What?"
"It goes from present tense to past tense. You didn't notice?"
"Oh. You ought to get that chair fixed. That creaking can
really get to you . . . "
"Mmn-hmm. Do you want to hear something I wrote myself,
when I was in my Depressed Dilettante stage? It's a
poem . . . wonder why I thought of it now. O well, you'll
love it, it's very earnest . . .

> 'I play life-death games
> like a goddess, grave and cold
> in the midst of your tricks: and
> only to endure you who
> come to me with your puzzles and
> progeny and dreams—
> you who come to me as an oracle
> when you need a whore
> and as a whore when you need an oracle—'

uh, I can't remember what comes after that."

Ernie, deciding not to worry about what he couldn't control
at the moment, and reminding himself that this was supposed
to be a vacation, tried to ease into the moment.
"Not bad . . . I used to write a little poetry once in a while
myself, when I was younger and had more time."
Very's laugh sounded haunted. "And what do you do with
your time now?"
She lit a cigarette, the flare of her match rearranging all the

lights and shadows in her face. It startled Ernie, who had just gotten used to the moonlight-hollowed cheeks and eyes.

"I'm in business."

"What kind?"

He smiled. "Well, let's just say I help keep the wheel turning."

"Oh. It's a secret. Good. I love secrets. They're the only things people don't bore their friends with. Just remember, Little Ernie, some secrets have these small bones that can lodge in your throat. Do chew well."

She smiled vacantly.

"Well, I'll bet you got a few secrets yourself."

Very seemed surprised. "Why no. Not one. Never been able to find one. I guess I just don't have the knack; I mean, I've looked and looked. Nothing. But I think it's swell if you have one . . . really."

She paused and drew on her cigarette, and scrutinized him. He frowned.

She continued: "I gather you're rather well-off. Financially, I mean."

His frown relaxed. "What makes you think so?"

She exhaled. "You can't afford not to be."

•   •

After a few minutes, Ernie decided that although talking with Very was offensive, it was less to be dreaded than total isolation. He stretched in his beachchair and absorbed the new night and wished that Very were soft and fuckable. He had unconsciously planned on at least one doe-eyed Mexican girl, dark and fluid, and instead he had drawn a New York crazy who had contempt, or something like it, in all the places he normally found respect. Or fear. Or affection. Or greed. He decided that she was simply a rotten judge of people and had no idea of who or what she was dealing with, in him.

He began to reconsider his first assessment of her as a liar; lunatic was gaining ground. And since he dealt with liars daily and lunatics rarely, he might as well enjoy the change of pace and company. For that matter, he might even fuck her, what the hell. He'd had plenty of actresses, but all shiny west-coast ambitious types, never a New York freak from the fringe element. Maybe after dinner, what with the wine and all . . . he thought of all the feminine barbed wire he'd seen dissolved in wine over the years; of all the claws withdrawn into soft fur and purring: what kittens women really were. The scratching, jumpy ones often ended up being the most lovable. Hostility was only one side of the coin, passion the other. And weirdness was only the flip side of imagination, which he, in bed, valued so highly. Although the way things were going today, it'd probably turn out that she had fleas in her hair or worse. But maybe he was just getting stuffy, old. For God's sake, she doesn't have fleas. Maybe he was just hungry. Always more critical when hungry. Where the hell is dinner? No wonder the place is empty, lousy service is a death blow to any business. Let's get the show on the road, Jack.

He picked up the walkie-talkie and pushed. "Say, listen, where the hell is—"
A series of loud clicks and buzzes interrupted him, then a tinny recording shrilled at him: several girls harmonizing in Spanish-accented English, alternately slurring and clipping their words, apparently not understanding the sense of what they were singing. An accordion whined an accompaniment, a drum kept missing the beat:

> "We are beezy-beezy-beezy
> At El 'Otel Cue Ess Grande
> We are pounin' cleanin' cookin'
> So eef service yoo are lookin'
> —FOR—
> Yool-'ave-to-wade-a-liddle-more!
> Ooo cha cha

152

Dough our staff ees 'ere to serve yoo
All da bes' dat yoo dee-serve yoo
Gringoes are too moch aggressive
Do yoo finally get our message
WEEEE————————————
are beezy-beezy-beezy—"

Ernie jammed the walkie-talkie into the sand, and found Very's laughter stupid and irritating. Can this woman do nothing but laugh inappropriately? He rubbed his hand over his forehead and eyes and listened for the surf-sounds. He knew that particular sound was said to be among the most calming to excited minds, raw nerves. He wondered why he only heard it when he listened for it. Deciding to salvage what he could from the situation, he turned his attention to Very and forced himself to smile, wondering if there was anything normal they could discuss—as the moon busied itself above them like a slow spirit, spreading light and deepening shadows.

"So. Even underground movie queens take vacations, eh?"
"O that's nice. It's stopped pouting. It wants to play again."
She was pretending her hand was a pistol. She was loading it with invisible bullets, polishing it, then finally aiming it at the moon's face.
"No, I'm not on—what was it you called it?—a vacation."
(She squinted down the barrel of her forefinger at the moon.)
"I'm here to make another weird and—click!—arty film which you of course will never go to . . . see the new crater I just made? Do you like it? I used a silencer so I wouldn't startle you with a sudden noise. See how considerate I really can be? I like you, Small Ern, I won't scare you with noises."
She let her pistol-hand fall into her lap, limp.
Ernie asked, "Well—then where is everybody? I mean the crew, the people you're making the movie with?" Maybe she was a lunatic liar.
"Tomorrow. I came a day early."

153

"Why?"

She seemed surprised. "To rest, obviously." He seemed to be weighing something. She continued, "Just think. But one brief night of bliss for us. What a grief. Then my career once again will claim me."

Her pistol-barrel was now resting on the arm of the rocker, aiming at Ernie, who said, "You mean you're all going to be making a movie right here, at this hotel?"

"Yeah. Maybe you can be in it, just for kicks, some little bit we can dream up—"

"Jesus."

"What's the matter, Little Ern? Shy?"

"Wouldn't be a good idea, business-wise."

"Oops. I think you just let the edge of your secret slip. Your slip's showing."

The gleam in his eye was somewhere between good-humor and threat. "Believing you have a little knowledge can be a dangerous thing."

"Did you just make that up?"

He looked steadily at her. She widened her eyes and let her hand fall, again, to her lap. Then she lit a cigarette and said, "I know nothing. I told you, I can't find a secret even when I try. So my life's very simple. I just stand in front of a camera and say somebody else's words. Of course, I'll admit I do contribute style . . . but that's less dangerous than knowledge, wouldn't you say? Style?"

Ernie grunted.

Very rocked. The chair creaked. Ernie cleared his throat and said,

"Sort of a professional free-spirit, eh?"

She looked away, bored suddenly and smoking.

He tried the walkie-talkie again: Static, then— "We are beezy-beezy-beezy-" Releasing the button, he swore quietly and sank back against the canvas, and tried to listen to the surf.

154

•   •   •

Time passed and the moon moved among its own mysteries in the dark. Water pounded the sand, shadows changed, and the two people breathed quietly, apart.

Then the shrill grating sound of wheels grinding their way through the sand interrupted the silence that was beginning to gnaw at Ernie, although Very hadn't noticed. She'd been deciding what to tell Alexander, tomorrow's director, about tonight: the basic truth, she thought, if the delivery could be funny enough; but if she didn't think of some good lines soon, she planned to start devising the most outrageous lie she could think of: to be told at tomorrow's dinner, with the whole cast and crew present, to be told with such good timing that everyone simply collapsed. To be told so well that Alexander lost the spotlight for a good fifteen minutes, which would cause him a great gnashing of teeth, which pride and cool would cause him to hide perfectly, which would cause him a further gnashing of teeth. The man she loved in a psychic wringer. Very's party.

The wheels' sound got louder, closer. She noticed. Both Ernie and Very looked toward the sound. It was M, almost hidden behind the wheeled table he was pushing. As he got even closer, they could see he was puffing and grinning and blinking back tears of fun. He was apparently very excited. He coughed a few times.

Now they could also see that it wasn't a dinner-table or picnic-table he was pushing, but a hospital stretcher—the kind that goes from patient's room to operating room. On its top was a huge silver tray-cover, almost as long and wide as the table/stretcher. Its polished curves gleamed in the light, its ornately carved handle glinting.

155

M dollied it into position next to Ernie, who was staring. M's hands clutched each other in anticipation, and Ernie said, "Jesus, M, we ordered a simple dinner for two, hours ago. You must have enough food under that thing for an army, and if you think you're gonna stick that on my bill, you're right out of your—"

Gathering all his strength, M whipped the gigantic cover up and off, giving himself the cue to begin singing: *"HAPPY HOLIDAY TO YOU HAPPY HOLIDAY TO YOU HAPPY HOLIDAY* SMALL FAT MOGUL *HAPPY—"*

Ernie stared at the table.

"What the fuck—?" Ernie stood up in one clean motion, something he'd been trying for years to learn.

M was fairly prancing around the table now, as he sang his horrible rendition of Happy Birthday, his voice nearly frightening in its cackling rasps and screeches. He was obviously beside himself with joy.

Very thought it was sweet to see M so spontaneous.

Ernie bellowed for the second time, *"What the fuck—"*

"—HOLIDAY TO YOU HAPPY—"

Ernie was pointing at the golden calf that was lying on the table. It was on its side, its hooves neatly tucked together, decorated with a few ribbon-curls. There were a hundred small pink and blue candles anchored and flickering on its topside—each one carefully stuck in its own drop of wax, all at different angles, due to the curvature of the calf. The gold-painted hide reflected each of the hundred points of light.

"—HOLIDAY TO YOU CURLY TYCOON *HAPPY—"*

The calf's eyes were open. It looked like it really didn't care.

Very was sulking: she lit a cigarette, crossed her legs, and said: "That's not a surprise, M. That's schtick."

"—TO YOU HAPPY HOLIDAY DIMPLY BABBITT *HA—"*

M, still singing and bobbing around in what seemed to Ernie a terrifying way, bent down to a shelf under the stretcher and brought out a small covered dish—also silver—and crunched

and hopped over to Very, and set it in her lap.
"—*PY HOLIDAY* CAPTAIN BIGSTUFF *HAPP*—"
She took the lid off. In the center of the dish was a
hypodermic syringe, full. She looked up at M.
"Now that's a surprise."
"—*HOLIDAY TO YOU*—"
Ernie said, "What the fuck—?" as Very gathered up her gauze
and searched her right thigh for a vein.
A thought flashed through Ernie: Now I'm sure of it, she's
gotta have fleas. Then a second thought: What the fuck am I
thinking about *that* for?
"—*IDAY* WORLDLY WANKER *HAP*—"
M bobbled towards Ernie now, who instinctively backed up a
step, lowering his head almost imperceptibly in unconscious
defense.
"—*HAPPY HOLIDAY* FLASHY WHARF RAT *HAPPY
HO*—"
M was so close, Ernie could smell the garlic on his breath.
M's old body jerked up and down, side to side, his bow-tie
askew now, a shirt button off, his coattails flapping like
frantic crow-wings behind him. He chugged and panted
inches away from Ernie, who was paralyzed in fascinated
repulsion.
"—*HAPPY HOLIDAY TO*—"
M's left arm drew into a praying mantis position, the hand a
knobby hook. Ernie stared and didn't breathe. The hand went
for Ernie's pants' pocket, diving in, a seagull plundering a
clam. M jiggled and bobbed. Ernie spit out— "What the hell
do you think you're doing?!"
"—*YOU* MORDANT MAGNATE *HAPPY HOLIDAY
TO*—"
M's claw withdrew, holding the balled-up dollar bill Ernie
had prepared earlier.
"—*HOLIDAY TO YOU*—"
Ernie shrieked, *"Do you realize who I am?"*
"—*AY* MONEYED SPITCURL *HAPPY HOL*—"
M, perhaps close to frenzy now, jagged over to the calf, and

157

lifting its limp tail with his right hand, shoved the paper ball into its anus with his left.

"—OH HAPPY HOLIDAY TO—"
He dropped the calf's tail with a little flourish, and it swung back and forth briskly, a tufted gold pendulum. All the calf's candles flickered in the soft breeze; hundreds of wax drops had fallen and were cooling on the shimmering hide, making tiny dull pockmarks. Very, having finished her dinner, rearranged her skirt, then sat and rocked slowly with the silver dish on her lap. It could've been a grey kitten, sleeping in a curl. She was humming low, bits of some strange melody.

Ernie tore his eyes off M, and looked at Very with new alarm; she looked soft and very fuckable now. He was disgusted. Then out of the corner of his eye he saw a flash of steel—he turned towards M, who had gotten a carving knife from the shelf in the stretcher, and still dancing frenetically, was cutting into the calf's back.

"—HOLIDAY BAD TASTE FLASHO BLUFFER—"
M carved a ragged chunk of meat and bone from the animal's neck and tossed it onto the platter that was now wedged in at an angle by the calf's head. He carved, or gouged, out another piece—this time from the calf's front leg. The two candles that were on the leg sputtered but kept burning upside down, as the meat was piled onto the platter. M went for a lower hind leg next, slashing off a tendony hunk.

Very began mumbling now, her head leaning back, her hands, palms up, in her lap, like the hands of saints in medieval paintings, like corks on water, like sorrows felt too late . . .
". . . and possibilities that . . . roll low into easy hands . . . . then go to powder . . . like old spices . . . dry and dusty . . . even love, that . . . eastside disaster . . ." (she chuckled quietly, a tape in slow motion) ". . . mysteries . . . ."

"—TO YOU HAPPY HOLIDAY—"
An ear with a candle tipping bounced on the growing meat

pile.

A hoof thudded on top of it, snuffing out the ear's candle. A thin slice from the hipbone, then one rib with all its three candles guttering.

Very's head rolled from side to side, slowly:

". . . mysteries and . . . magic, ah, now . . . well, that's . . . they circle around and . . . croon at me . . . those sphinxes and crystals . . . those minor deceptions . . . but, o mama . . . it's okay . . . it's all so okay . . . watching . . . things . . . curve up, hoping . . . and circle down . . . burning . . ."

"—HOLIDAY I SAY O HAPPY HOLIDAY—"

The ragged old woman stood quietly at the water's edge, and felt it rush, again and again, around her ankles. She felt it pull the sand from beneath her heels, felt the breeze travel through the tatters she wore hanging from her ancient body, felt the stars and moon slide in formation, felt the time.

She watched and heard the people up on the beach: the old man dancing and shrieking, the short man standing in confused rage, the young woman rocking and speaking low, talking high.

She tasted all their needs and furies, every bitterness and pleasure, each small triumph and loss over the others and themselves, she tasted their tears. She knew their lives and had no opinion, she played no favorites. She said, "All to dust but the eye, winkless . . . and a few things that turn."

Then she laughed.

FICTION COLLECTIVE

books in print:

Reruns by Jonathan Baumbach
Museum by B. H. Friedman
Twiddledum Twaddledum by Peter Spielberg
Searching for Survivors by Russell Banks
The Secret Table by Mark Mirsky
98.6 by Ronald Sukenick
The Second Story Man by Mimi Albert
Things in Place by Jerry Bumpus
Reflex and Bone Structure by Clarence Major
Take It or Leave It by Raymond Federman
The Talking Room by Marianne Hauser
The Comatose Kids by Seymour Simckes
Althea by J. M. Alonso
Babble by Jonathan Baumbach
Temporary Sanity by Thomas Glynn
Ø Null Set and Other Stories by George Chambers
Amateur People by Andrée Connors
Moving Parts by Steve Katz
Statements 1, an anthology of new fiction (1975)
Statements 2, an anthology of new fiction (1977)

FICTION COLLECTIVE   NEW YORK